Beach Wedding
on the
Rocks

Beach Wedding on the Rocks

Maddie Evans

Philangelus Press
Boston, MA USA

Publisher: Philangelus Press
ISBN: 978-1-942133-48-3
Cover art by Black Widow Books
Editing by Jane Lebak

Also by Maddie Evans:

The Brighthead Running Club Romances
The Castleton String Quartet Romances
Matchmaking the Midwife
Meeting Up with the Mason
Drake (Last Man Standing)

CHAPTER ONE

What a revolting development.

On the steps of his apartment, Noah Szymczak paused mid-shuffle through the day's mail, staring at what had to be a wedding invitation. The last name and address in the corner meant it came from no one other than Dan Bluett, inveterate prankster and life-ruiner. And former friend.

Well, would-be former friend, if only Noah had ever actually told him off. He hadn't. Just moved away.

Still.

With five minutes remaining of his lunch break before he'd return to his home office, Noah opened the envelope to reveal another envelope—which was as good a metaphor for Dan as anything Noah could have come up with. Inside that was a slice of hefty cardstock emblazoned with birds and ribbon hearts, and short choppy lines that Dan and Skye "request the honor of your presence."

Oh, and how cute—they had a wedding hashtag.

#BluettSkyes.

Of course Dan would want Noah there to witness him get married—when in effect, the last thing Dan had done before leaving for college was make sure Noah wouldn't. Wouldn't get married to Elsie Jenner, that was.

The wedding would be in Brighthead, Maine, so Dan hadn't gone far afield. Or maybe the location was because of Skye, his bride who'd been a year behind them at Brighthead High School.

Easy excuse. Noah had moved four hours from Brighthead, and in the immortal words of his father, "I didn't leave anything there." Noah could have opened the third envelope, which undoubtedly contained the RSVP card, but instead he used his phone to scan the QR code and fill out the website form. "Sorry, won't be able to make it."

After that, he had one minute left before logging back in to his job. He spent that minute the best way he could: dropping that invitation into the shredder. It entered as a bad memory and emerged as sharp-edged diamonds. *And that is enough of that.*

———◆———

At least, that would have been enough of that, if Noah hadn't awakened the next morning to a text from a number he hadn't seen in eight years. Timestamped at two o'clock in the morning. From Elsie Jenner.

Elsie?

"You had better get here for that wedding."

CHAPTER TWO

Szymczak had better get here for that wedding, and that was all Elsie had to say about it.

Except she'd said so many things about it already, from incoherent shrieking when Skye had texted about Noah's RSVP decline, to a two-hour running monologue while Elsie stress-cleaned the entire beach house, to nasty things muttered at her dishes, to—

Well, to two o'clock in the morning when her heart finally overflowed the monologue into her fingertips. Before she thought better, she'd had her phone in her hands, texting Szymczak he'd better get himself to his hometown for that wedding or so help her, she'd track him down and drag him back by his gorgeous hair.

Sending messages at two o'clock in the morning was not, in fact, Elsie's best trait. Staring at the sent message at six a.m., eyes stinging, she had to admit as much.

Monologues in the head, though...they had to go

somewhere. She should have texted it to Skye. Except Skye wouldn't have understood just how much Elsie hated Dan Bluett. Because, again, Elsie hadn't really said anything specific to Skye. Not even in a text sent at two o'clock in the morning.

The text to Szymczak said "delivered," so maybe Elsie would get lucky. Maybe this wasn't his phone number any longer. Maybe it would remain forever thus—delivered but unread—or maybe his father had taken over the phone number and would see it, realize Elsie had lost her mind, and delete it before—

—It turned to "read."

Nausea settled so deep in Elsie's stomach that she couldn't even reach for her coffee.

Welcome back into her life, Noah Szymczak. To whom she only referred by last name, now. Now, after he'd stomped on her heart by being a self-absorbed mockery of a human being who knew how to look contrite when he wanted to, and then knew how to do exactly whatever he pleased the next time the opportunity came up. Which lack of character Dan had revealed in its full glory after high school graduation with that oh-so-funny "prank" on Elsie's eighteenth birthday.

Was twenty-six-year-old Noah still as warm-eyed and good-looking as he'd been at eighteen? Did he still have that tousled brown hair and innocent expression? Would he try again to melt Elsie's heart by apologizing from the very bottom of his soul for making a well-intentioned mistake that surely, surely!, even Elsie could see he'd done with her very best interests in mind?

She snorted. Yes, the reason not to call him "Noah" was pretty clear, wasn't it? Because the minute Elsie used his first name, she remembered how much she'd loved him back then, when she'd known with full conviction that he was her perfect match, and they'd each promised the other they'd be "the one" for the rest of their lives. "Noah" was warm and cute and smart and amazing, whereas "Szymczak" was more full of himself than he was full of consonants. And—and this was the best part—in Elsie's head, she intentionally pronounced it wrong. Because she might (might) warm up to "Shim-chuck." But "Sim-zack" was the name of a supervillain with no justification in his origin story.

For the final bit of zing, Noah hated it when people pronounced it Sim-zack.

Elsie returned to her coffee. She had work to go to: horses and therapists and clients awaited. No matter what Szymczak did with Elsie's text, Skye was still getting married at the beach house in six weeks, and there was work to be done for that, too.

It was just—Dan broke them up for a prank. It would be fitting if Elsie could get some kind of payback against Dan before he got married. Breaking up Elsie and Noah had meant so little to Dan that the jerk didn't even realize how much Elsie still wished he'd get kicked by a horse into a bottomless pit, then be stung by magical air jellyfish all the way down.

If there was anyone on earth whose existence bothered her more than Szymczak's, it was Dan Bluett's.

As she set her empty mug in the dishwasher, a ping stopped Elsie's heart.

She edged back to the table. Szymczak had replied. "Why had I better go to this wedding?"

Because it's not fair if you don't. Because you should have just as much of a grievance against Dan as I do. Because it's not right that I have to handle this all on my own when I had to clean up the mess alone eight years ago, and I was the one you hurt.

She couldn't make her fingers type any of that. But she also couldn't make them type, "Never mind. Slink back into your burrow."

What burrow was Szymczak even calling home right now? For all she knew, he might be texting from the International Space Station.

A second text appeared. "I would have thought you wouldn't want me there."

Her thoughts unstuck, and she replied: "Clearly I do."

She shouldn't have responded. She should have left the ice wall in place, but the second she hit send, the emotions flooded back. Szymczak needed to come here. He was avoiding her, even if he was trying to make his avoidance sound like chivalry, as if he was thinking of her feelings over his own, (eight years too late for that!) but really, it was nothing more than cowardice.

He texted, "Why?"

Her hands trembled. "Because you owe me. And we both owe Dan."

Silence.

She added, "They're having a cute little wedding on the rocky beach, and he thinks his life is perfect. We need to get payback."

Szymczak replied, "With eight years of interest?"

Oh, yes! He was getting it, now. "With interest. You come here, get back at him for what he did on my birthday, and we even the score."

Szymczak replied, "Revenge is a dish best served cold?"

She replied, "Eight years. Stone cold."

"I'm thinking more, on-the-rocks."

She glanced out the kitchen window at the rocky beach.

He added, "You know, like on ice?"

"I got it," she replied. "It's just that, it was dumb."

"Wow. Harsh."

She snorted.

He added, "You never liked my puns."

"I liked your good puns," she replied.

He sent a sad emoji, and her mouth twitched in self-defense as she snickered. *No. No, no, no.* He should not be making her laugh. He should be on his knees, penitent, devising ways they could be retaliating at Dan for hurting her. Not trying to be cute.

Except maybe Szymczak wasn't trying to be cute. Maybe he still was, actually, cute.

Blast.

Szymczak said, "How'd you even know I RSVP'd?"

"I'm the Maid of Honor. I had Skye invite you, so she told me when you said no. Go back to the website and change your RSVP. Then get here a week before the wedding so we can set something up."

"A whole week? Are you planning to saw off the peninsula and sink Brighthead into the sea?" Then, "I need the website address. I shredded the invitation."

She replied, "You were serious about not coming!"

"Dan messed up my life, too. Why would I want to celebrate his wedding?"

A momentary hollowness fluttered inside Elsie. The last time she'd seen Noah, his brown eyes had been soft. Confused. Imploring.

Dan messed up both their lives. But given how Skye was Elsie's best friend, it couldn't be Elsie getting revenge. At least, not Elsie alone.

"I'm in," Szymczak texted. "But let's plan, because if we're pranking the master prankster, I want to go big."

CHAPTER THREE

Through the window, Noah laid eyes on Elsie for the first time in eight years.

It wasn't quite laying eyes on her, not yet. It was just that he'd been pacing the tiny rental unit, jumping at every sound, glancing out the window every forty-two seconds (rough estimate) and then finally he'd heard an engine slow and a car pull into the driveway, and *this* glance had been rewarded by seeing a car and then seeing the driver and finally seeing it was her.

Which was—wow.

He whipped open the door and then tried against all hope to look relaxed, as if he weren't about to stick his finger into a mousetrap and get snapped.

Elsie slid out of the sedan looking amazing—lithe and poised and well put-together. She was wearing well-broken-in riding boots that rode right up her calves and her tight jeans. That made sense: her online profiles said she worked with horses, of all things. Except she was tiny. She always had been, so how could she face down a thousand pounds of raw force every day?

She met his gaze at the door, and the steel in her eyes answered that question, at least.

She tilted her head, and some strands of her straight dark hair had escaped her low ponytail to graze her jawline. She still reminded him of an elf with that sure stance and angular body.

The way she studied him, she was probably taking the same kind of inventory, only it didn't seem as if her opinion were anywhere near as positive.

"Thanks for coming here," Noah managed.

"I should say the same. You're the one who boarded a plane, rented a car, and found a rental unit." She approached. "Can we go inside?"

Oh, right. Noah re-booted his brain and opened the door.

It was nothing to speak of. He'd found it on a vacation rental website, just the bottom floor of a family home with a minuscule kitchen, a tiny bedroom, and a bathroom with a shower stall. It was, however, cheap and available—awesome characteristics considering it was the middle of summer, and Noah hadn't even intended to come here five weeks ago.

Elsie's nose wrinkled. Before she could declare the place was a dump, Noah held a finger over his lips. He leaned closer, breathing in *sotto voz*, "I'm pretty sure the owner can hear everything we say."

Elsie followed his gaze to the heat register over the cold woodstove. "Ah. Like my grandmother's house."

Her grandmother not only had heat registers that allowed the slightest sound to travel the entire length of the house, but she also had a suspicious streak as wide as Penobscot Bay and ears more sensitive than an owl tracking a mouse through a corn field. Any sound that hinted at a kiss, and she'd be down the stairs in a heartbeat with a tray of hot chocolate and cookies, and then she'd sit with Noah and Elsie to eat them.

Noah said, "Too bad there aren't any cookies."

"Don't say that too loudly. My grandmother may drive over from Flower Farms Apartments with a thermos of hot chocolate." Elsie carefully settled on the metal chair at the table that only wobbled a bit. It was big enough for one person to eat breakfast, provided that breakfast consisted of a muffin and a cup of coffee, and nothing else. Whether it wobbled because the legs were uneven or the floor was, Noah couldn't say.

In fact, there was nearly nothing he could say. Eight years of silence compounded in his head into confusion about what it is you should say to the woman you ought to have been planning your five year wedding anniversary with, maybe with a couple of kids. Instead he only knew what she did for a living because he'd found it on a professional website. "So...hippotherapy?" He raised an eyebrow. "How do you get the hippos to lie down on a couch and tell you about their mothers?"

She raised an eyebrow right back at him. "Really, Szymczak? *Hippos?*"

Noah added, "Did you study that on the hippo-campus?"

Elsie looked tolerant. "Are you done?"

Noah shook his head. "I still have lines about Hippocrates, the Hippocratic Oath, and the hippodrome."

"Wow, the last eight years have totally flown by, and I see why, now." She wrinkled her nose at him. "You do know the hippo in hippotherapy is horses, right?"

Noah had learned that about two minutes after he'd seen it on her profile, when he'd clicked the link to her employer's website. He steepled his fingers. "So, young Trigger, tell me about your sire."

She rubbed her chin. "You were dreaming about hay. Perhaps that's symbolic of the fact that you're always hungry." Then she said, "Oh, no, actually it means the horses are well-adjusted, and it's the riders who need the therapy."

Noah said, "I wouldn't have pegged you as the

psychiatry type."

"Because it's not. We're physical therapy." She sat taller as she spoke. "The motion of the horses simulates the motion of the human pelvis during walking, so someone who's had a stroke, or someone with cerebral palsy, can work out their hips and thoracic spine without any kind of impact or having to support their own weight."

Noah straightened. "Oh, I did have that wrong. I thought you were using horses as emotional support animals to help nonverbal kids learn to talk."

"Some practitioners do, but that's not my area. I help the patient get on and off the horse safely, and then we walk around the arena at a pace geared toward helping the patient calibrate their own movements."

Noah leaned forward. "That sounds like an awesome career. You and a bunch of horses, and parents giving you gifts at the end of the year because you helped their little one learn to walk."

"I'm not the real therapist. Dr. Morgan gets the accolades while I'm hanging the tack in the back room. Elsie tightened her mouth. "Just the way I want it to be. So," and she cocked her head to force a change of subject, "plans?"

Noah didn't want to talk about plans. He wanted to say, "You look really good." Because she did. She looked just like he'd have imagined she would look nowadays—bolder and stronger than in high school. Shedding him had done her a world of good, and that hurt. She'd said she had to break up with him because it was better that way, but why did she have to be right?

He steeled himself against his own feelings as he pulled out his tablet computer. "We've got any number of targets for pranks, but what kind of revenge are we looking for? One-for-one payback would mean pulling a prank big enough to call off the wedding."

Elsie's eyes widened. "Are you serious?"

"Considering he broke us up when we were talking about marriage, that's what full payback would mean. I can't imagine you're down for that, so let's clarify. Are we inconveniencing him? Getting photographs of him with a hooker? Damaging property?"

"No property damage. Especially because the property in question is my mother's beach house." Elsie crossed her long legs, and Noah kept his eyes riveted to the tablet so he wouldn't end up checking her out. "No hookers. I'm going to say nothing that damages the house, and no glitter."

He looked up. "No glitter bombs?"

"No, Szymczak, no glitter bombs."

Noah flinched. "Sim-zack?"

She rewarded him with a smirk. Not cool. Elsie leaned back and folded her arms. "We're operatives. Officers call one another by their last names."

"If we're both officers, that would make you my partner, and you un-partnered me...Jenner." He narrowed his eyes as she narrowed hers. "You and I are the opposite of law enforcement officers."

She looked mischievous. "We're spies, infiltrating behind enemy lines."

Noah huffed. "Not spies. More like, we're pulling off a heist."

"Heist-ers need code names. Szymczak is a good code name."

"Yes, since it's not actually my last name. When you're captured, no one will guess it's me."

Elsie snorted. "*Anyhow*, there's another consideration. My mother wants to maybe start renting out the beach house for weddings every summer. So we can't trash Dan and Skye's reception. My mother needs good photos and good reviews."

Noah's nose wrinkled. "Yeah, that's—well, it's limiting."

"Also, we can't touch Skye."

Noah said, "You're just saying that because you want me to reply that *Skye's the limit*."

"No, Szymczak. I'm saying that because she's still my best friend, and she's had her heart broken in the past."

Elsie looked aside. "She's already nervous about the wedding. I don't want her to feel like I'm betraying her, so she shouldn't really find out I'm involved. That's why no entrapment with hooker photos. I just want to get back at Dan."

Noah laid his tablet on the table and folded his arms. "Look, you're making this impossible. You had me fly up here so we could get revenge on Dan. No problem—Dan deserves it. But you're tying our hands every way possible. How do you suggest we prank the wedding couple without pranking either the bride or the wedding?"

Elsie recoiled, looking stung. "You were always the prank mastermind. I thought you'd have some ideas."

"I do have ideas! They're ideas about how to prank a wedding. Not ideas about how to prank a wedding without pulling off any pranks. Nothing that leave residue, and no pranks the bride will notice, and nothing that involves you, leaves us with painting 'save me' on the soles of Dan's shoes, and I'm not doing that because that would be at Skye's expense."

Elsie stared at the floor. "I could write on the soles of *her* shoes. 'Dan's a jerk.'"

"Perfect, except they aren't having a religious ceremony and therefore won't be kneeling." Noah folded his arms. "Something's got to give.

Elsie's pout was a thing of beauty. She put her all into the pout without seeming to.

Noah said, "If you're dating someone, you could have him propose to you during the reception."

Elsie said, "Except first, I'm not dating anyone, and second, proposing at someone else's wedding is not a prank. It's just tacky attention-whoring."

Noah nodded. "And you're the opposite of an attention-whore. So, let's get creative. You have access to the house where they're staying."

Elsie's head popped up. "We can get into their luggage."

Noah pointed at her. "Now you're thinking. We probably have full access to their electronics. Or we shortly will."

Elsie tilted her head. Again, she looked cute, and Noah forcibly angled his face away as he picked up the tablet off the table.

She said, "What would that get us?"

"Access to literally everything. Didn't I tell you I work in cybersecurity?"

Elsie choked. "Wait, what?"

Noah added, "I bet one or the other of them hasn't changed their phone code since senior year of high school."

Elsie said, "And here I was thinking of something like filling the getaway car with plastic balls."

"Too boring. By the time we're done, Dan's going to wonder if he's in the same reality as the rest of us."

Elsie sat up taller. "Nothing says we're limited to the wedding day."

Noah's eyebrows shot up. "What other events are there?"

"There's the wedding rehearsal and the rehearsal dinner. There's the bachelor party. There's the final tux fitting. Um…" She shook her head. "Skye and Dan invited the whole wedding party out here for the week so they can have fun ahead of time. She's picking up her dress. No, Szymczak," Elsie interrupted before Noah could even draw breath. "We aren't doing anything to the dress. Just Dan."

"Fine." Noah grinned. "But I want their schedule. And then, I want to hit every event."

CHAPTER FOUR

Dan was every bit as annoying as ever as Elsie entered the beach house. "Szymczak!"

Elsie stepped aside while Dan (who pronounced it correctly) strode right up to Szymczak and chucked him on the shoulder. "Man, you're looking great! So glad you were able to make it out here."

Szymczak didn't look like someone delighted by reuniting with his best friend after eight years. "Thanks for the invite."

Elsie slipped into the kitchen while Dan and Noah (Szymczak, blast it—she couldn't slip already) caught up. Skye wasn't in evidence, so Elsie got some water from the dispenser and stood by the kitchen window.

Brighthead Bay lay before her, wavelets lapping against the rocks beyond the deck. At the end of the week, they'd hold the ceremony on those rocks, then the reception in and around the house.

Although Elsie would give Skye anything she asked, this ask hadn't been easy. The beach house was everything Mom had worked for during twenty long Maine winters. They'd lived in a cramped and drafty bungalow, and then finally Mom was able to purchase something right on the shore. Alone. No help. She'd saved and invested, and now this house felt like a sign of victory. When Mom moved inland so she wouldn't have to winter over in Brighthead any longer, Elsie had stayed behind—stayed in Mom's beautiful house without Mom in it anymore.

After which, Skye had felt entitled to use it. To which Mom had said, "I don't go there every week, so maybe we can rent it out and do more weddings there?" Leaving Elsie trapped because once again, something that meant so much to her heart had been just a practicality for everyone else.

Mom didn't see the house as an accomplishment: she saw it as property.

Elsie slid open the glass doors and stepped onto the deck, into the ocean breeze. She adored that particular rocky oceanfront scent she'd come to associate with coastal Maine: the salt, the shellfish, the seaweed, the lichen. Some of it must be decay, but as a whole, it smelled like home. Maybe that's why Skye wanted her wedding near the water. Water was always moving, always new. Waves came in, and because the action was under the surface, they didn't seem to leave again even as the next arrived.

The motion steadied her, despite Dan being in the house. She'd tolerate that jerk for Skye's sake, but it was easier to tolerate Dan when Elsie could keep her eyes on the water and the moving clouds, where she could feel the air around her.

If Mom really did begin to rent out this house for people's events, Elsie would have to move. She snickered to herself—maybe she could sign a lease on that rat-hole of an apartment Szymczak had gotten for the week? Then, on the first of the month, she could turn off her alarm and immediately hear the landlord in his or her own kitchen saying, "Rent's due."

The door slid open, and she braced herself in case it was Dan—but really, she'd need to brace herself against Noah, too. (Szymczak. Hold fast.)

It was Noah with his laptop tucked under his arm. "I'm just going to work outside for a while."

Elsie said, "Do you need the Wi-Fi password?"

"I'm going to need to access your router, and then I'm going to need you to promise not to call the police on me." He laughed. "But—well, it's all in good fun, as Dan just reminded me."

"Some fun."

"Well," he said, not looking quite at her as he opened the laptop, "I'm not looking for good fun. I'm waiting for great fun. Oh, thanks."

She'd just cranked open the umbrella to shade the laptop screen. "I figured you'd be assisted by being able to see whatever it is you're doing."

"It helps, yes. Anyhow, I asked Dan to show me something on social media, and once he was checking his socials, he got lost in his phone, so I slipped out. It's a pretty easy trap to spring. What's the Wi-Fi password?"

She said, "WeBoughtThisHouseIn2021."

He stopped. "That's not a bad password."

"I know, right? It's long, and it's got numbers, and we can remember it."

Skye bounced onto the deck, beaming. "I cannot believe you're here!" He barely got out of his chair before she was hugging him. "It's been ages! I'm so glad Elsie talked you into coming."

"It's good to be back." Szymczak even seemed like he meant it.

"Did Elsie drive you around so you could see all the new stuff? They cleaned up the town green, and you should see the new field at the high school."

Noah had worked hard to leave Brighthead—and he hadn't ever played high school sports. Elsie couldn't imagine he'd be even slightly interested in the new field. "He's only just gotten here," she said.

"Well, you've got a few days. You'll have to go with Dan to all the things he's doing with the groomsmen. They've booked a whale watch, and of course the bachelor party."

Noah kept his face impassive. "Elsie mentioned those."

She grinned. "Dan's so excited you were finally coming back."

Dan joined them on the deck, and Noah shut his laptop. "I'm sorry to break up the party, but I just got an email from my boss about an incursion. Elsie, where's a good place for me to work for a bit?"

Elsie said, "There's a computer desk in the small bedroom on the first floor, toward the front of the building."

"Awesome, thanks." He smiled. "Let me know if you guys come up with plans for dinner," and he went inside.

Half an hour later, Skye glanced at her phone and giggled. She slipped her arm around Dan's waist. "I know you're my sweetie, but a sweet potato?"

Brow furrowed, Dan said, "Huh?"

Elsie leaned over and took a look at Skye's phone screen. Dan's social media status had been updated: "Sometimes when I get insomnia, I paint myself orange and lie in the neighbor's lawn to pretend I'm a sweet potato."

Elsie bit her lip, grinning. Operation Payback was off to a good start.

CHAPTER FIVE

Elsie and Skye drove to the bridal salon with Skye wide-eyed and jittery.

"Last time around taught me I should be relaxed." Skye adjusted the window up and down, seeking the perfect spot where it let in the air without whipping her hair all over the place. "I was super stressed when I was marrying Alan, and you know, maybe that's part of why he bolted?"

"He bolted because he was a loser." Alan hadn't bothered letting anyone on Skye's side of the family know he was skipping town, not even on the morning of the wedding. His whole side was there at the rehearsal dinner, and the next morning, none of them showed. Alan had fled to California.

Szymczak, at least, had only fled to another corner of New England.

Skye made a brave face, a lie utterly betrayed by how her hands never stopped moving. "This week, I'm going to chill out. As long as at the end of the day we're married, then it worked."

Elsie chuckled as she slowed for a light. "Surely you have higher expectations. If you only wanted to be married, you could have gone to a courthouse."

"I want to have a party, and I don't want to stress about it." Hence why Skye had offloaded the stress onto Elsie and her mother. Doubtless also why she still hadn't found the perfect level for the window. "I want the white dress and the tuxedo and the tall cake. But perfection? It would be misrepresenting everything about me to have a picture-perfect wedding."

The light changed, and Elsie pulled onto Route 1. "That's a good way to think about it."

Skye in no way thought of it like that. Skye was terrified and jittery and anticipating the sword of Damocles would impale her a second time. Instead she sounded like someone repeating a mantra she didn't believe, probably something she found in a bridal article. "Something's going to go wrong, so why not ride the wave when it does?"

With Dan as the groom, things were going to go wrong. Most especially because he *was* going to show up and exchange vows with Skye.

After getting a bunch of texts calling him Sweet Potato, and Kevin (Dan's best man) texting with, "I Yam impressed," Dan had changed all his social media passwords. Which was awesome, but was not going to help him escape Szymczak's grasp. He'd cracked it once. He likely had all the new ones within five minutes.

Dan was at the house, with Szymczak also staying put in the computer room, where he was theoretically working. (Well, he was working. Working both on Operation Payback and Operation Paying Job.)

At the bridal salon, Skye was so excited to see her gown for the final fitting. "I think I've lost five pounds in the last week," she admitted. People talked about water weight, but Skye probably lost it all in adrenaline. "Please let that dress still fit!"

"That's why we're here." Their hostess exuded calm as she escorting them to a fitting room. Skye's dress was already hanging on a rolling cart.

Elsie would never have let Szymczak prank this dress. Skye deserved to feel like a princess, even if for only a day. Although she hadn't blown the bank on a single-use outfit, she still had chosen it with care and adored the fit and the beads and the lace. Paired with her veil, that dress was going to look magnificent.

It was a different style than the first time around, though. Whether Skye realized or not, her nerves were dictating policy.

Elsie sat on a padded bench across a fitting room large enough to park a Honda Accord. Some dresses must have a jaw-dropping crinoline to make that necessary, or maybe most brides arrived with seven bridesmaids, their mother, the groom's mother, and a photographer—all of whom needed to see the bride now-now-now.

Well, it wasn't like Elsie had any upcoming chance to do this herself, so she might as well sit back and enjoy.

Skye stripped out of her clothes and into shapewear that got glued to her body. The tailor helped her into the dress, and that's when Skye's phone caught Elsie's eye.

Elsie snuck the phone off the bench and into her lap before the dress was all the way over Skye's head. Elsie plunked her own phone back on the cushion, and now if Skye didn't look too closely, it would seem like her phone was right where she'd left it.

Now for the question Szymczak had posed last night: had Skye changed her passcode since eighth grade, when she used her hot lunch number as the PIN?

3-6-7-1.

The home screen resolved. Elsie was in.

She went right to the text app. While the tailor buttoned a row of buttons down Skye's back, Elsie texted Dan, "I forgot we need a hydrangea brace. Can you be a sweetie and get one? Any of the florists should have it, or maybe the garden center at the hardware store."

Sent.

Elsie added, "Getting fitted now. You're the best."

Sent.

She deleted both texts, then dropped the phone into her lap as Skye faced her. "You look gorgeous," Elsie breathed.

"You think so?" Skye's cheeks were flushed. "This isn't the kind of dress I envisioned when I started, but when I tried it on, it just worked."

Despite all her worries, Skye's dress fit like a glove. She had bare shoulders but elbow-length sleeves, and the skirt flared at the knees. It had a long row of buttons up the back, and lace roses climbing her left side.

Walked around Skye to make sure the hem was even all around, Elsie said, "You didn't envision a groom like Dan, either, and yet here you are."

Skye beamed. "Touché. He was such a goof-off in high school."

Elsie gestured at the dress with her chin. "He'd better not spill red wine on your dress for the laughs."

Skye sighed. "He changed during college. Although he still loves a good prank."

Elsie slipped the button to silence notifications on Skye's phone. "Some things never change."

Skye looked at herself in the mirror. "That's a good thing. Next week, everything else changes. But we're still going to be the same, and that's a comfort."

CHAPTER SIX

Dan was already irritated at the beginning of his bachelor party, and Noah worked hard at keeping a straight face. Fortunately, a degree in cybersecurity was more of a law enforcement degree than a computer science degree, so in addition to digital forensics and Linux server administration, Noah had learned to sound baffled on discovering his partner in crime had sent their target searching all of Brighthead for an important wedding implement that didn't exist.

And then had kept the bride away from home for the rest of the afternoon, so the bride and groom couldn't compare notes.

The restaurant had assigned the bachelor party a function room with music, brighter lights than the dining room, and wide windows overlooking the ocean. There were no candles on the tables. Dan knew his set: his idiot friends (of whom Noah once considered himself Member

Number One) would have been setting fire to the utensils before the evening was over. Instead there were fishbowls with mechanical fish, and Noah photographed those to figure out how he could get one for himself. It was just a shame he couldn't hack the fish and make them all blow bubbles at the same time if the night featured any speeches.

Noah reconnected with high school friends, as easy as any man with an innocent conscience. Best Man Kevin was a former high school friend as well—another of Dan's partners in crime, but one who'd never had any imagination when it came to pranks. He'd thought dousing people with a bucket of water was high humor. By sheer luck, Noah had worked one summer at this exact venue, so he knew the manager and spent time catching up with him, too.

It was one of the area's nicest restaurants. Ahead of the wedding, Dan and Skye had arranged a tour of "Brighthead's Greatest Hits." Everything they'd set up sounded thoughtful and well-planned.

Which almost made it a shame that Noah would have to ruin it all.

Noah's phone buzzed. It was Elsie, but he'd named her contact Jen (short for Jenner) because if Dan got hold of the phone, Noah didn't want to inadvertently betray her. This was, in all likelihood, too much security, but Noah couldn't let go of everything he'd learned. While he didn't consider himself a criminal, after all that training, he ought to follow a criminal's best practices.

"Jen" had texted, "You must keep me updated."

He replied, "Anything special?"

She sent, "Of course."

Sure, be enigmatic. Whatever happened could surprise them all at the same time.

Servers meandered with platters of hors d'oeuvres, and Noah took one off the tray. It looked like a mini caprese, but instead of a tomato, the mozzarella and basil were toothpick-stabbed through a strawberry.

This was odd. Tasty, but odd. It had a lemony tang. He grabbed another before the server moved too far away.

The next appetizer that came through was a crostini with what may have been goat cheese, and another slice of strawberry.

Grinning, Noah slipped away from his current position and got up close to Dan just as the servers approached with the first tray. Dan glanced at it, looked irritated, and sent the server away.

Noah said to Dan, "I'm glad you chose this place. It's gone upscale from when I washed their dishes."

"Probably got upscale because they got rid of you." Laughing, Dan turned to the next server holding a tray. "What on earth?"

It was the strawberry crostini. Noah took another one. "This is delicious. Try one!"

Dan made a face. "I hate strawberries. This isn't what I picked for the appetizer."

Noah tilted his head. "Weird. I wonder why they subbed it."

Dan shrugged. "There's a whole meal coming up, though. I might as well save room."

When they were seated, the first course was a salad with strawberries. The next course was a cold strawberry soup.

Noah texted photos of every dish to Elsie, who wherever she was must have been frantically deleting them off her phone so Skye wouldn't see.

The main entree choices were either a chicken taco with strawberry salsa, or pork chops with a balsamic strawberry glaze. Vegetarians could have a strawberry and avocado tostada.

Noah texted Elsie, "You outdid yourself."

Elsie texted back, "I'm not playing."

Across the room, Dan threw his napkin onto his seat and stalked into the kitchen.

Noah could already predict that the dessert would require no fewer than six gallons of strawberries—maybe a strawberry pie with strawberry ice cream on the side, or strawberry mousse topped with strawberry whipped cream.

Dan returned from the kitchen, scanning the room until that laser-like glare settled on Noah.

Noah dug into his strawberry-chicken taco. Which was fantastic, by the way.

Dan pulled over a chair and sat halfway between Noah and Kevin. "You enjoying the food?"

Noah said, "It's all been amazing."

"Glad to hear that. They're bringing me a burger and fries in about five minutes." Dan called to one of the guests across the table, "Ted, have you met Noah Szymczak?"

"We were just talking," said the other guest, whose name Noah had already forgotten.

Dan said, "We all met in high school drama club. I always loved a good prank, and Noah did, too. We were partners in crime."

Noah beamed. "That we were."

Kevin said, "Hey. Me, too!"

Dan said, "Yes, you, too. But you always got caught. Once Noah came along, the teachers had a harder time pinning things on us, and it was entirely because of Noah's twisted genius brain."

Noah turned to Dan. "I can't take all the credit. You whipped up your own share of stunts."

"Oh, but yours were genius." Turning back to Ted, Dan continued, "Noah swiped the math teacher's car keys during lunch, and we moved his car to another part of the parking lot."

Noah said, "Dan's leaving out his part. We got four sets of keys, and we moved all the cars around so all these teachers were in the wrong spots. We did it five days running."

Dan grinned. "Exactly! One Christmas, Noah figured out how to stage a fake food drive, using the school mass-email system and flyers on the school letterhead. We convinced everyone to store all the nonperishable food in the vice principal's office while she was on her honeymoon, so it ended up being wall-to-wall cans on her first day back from vacation."

Fighting a pang, Noah forced a laugh. That hadn't been his idea—it had been Elsie's. "The VP was so angry, but fortunately, no one could remember who exactly it was who started instructing people to put the food in there. Once a few people knew, they kept telling everybody else. That's how these things work: no one remembers who first said something they assume is common knowledge. And then Dan and I were rewarded with a half day off from school when we volunteered to drive ten thousand cans to the Brighthead Food Cupboard."

Dan beamed. "All my friends were pranksters, but the others? They got caught. Or they had dumb ideas, like Kevin here who set the clocks fifteen minutes ahead so he'd get out of class sooner."

Kevin huffed. "It worked."

Noah said, "They should have expected as much when they locked two hundred smart kids in a building for six and a half hours a day."

Dan said, "And then our senior prank? Epic. Eight classes since then have tried to beat it—and no one has."

Leaning forward, Dan rested his forearms on Noah's and Kevin's seats. Garnering attention was a skill Dan had perfected during drama club: everyone at the table was watching him. Elsie would have withered away and died under that much scrutiny.

Dan continued, but instead of spooling out the saga of their senior prank, he said, "It always bothered me that my best pranks were Noah's ideas, but after the end of senior year, I pulled my own epic prank. Noah was dating this sweet but super-shy girl named Elsie. She was part of drama club, too, but she hated the spotlight—so she always worked as stage manager. We couldn't ever get her to set foot in front of the curtain, but Noah was head over heels for her. He and she got voted the high school's cutest couple, and who could resist that target?"

With a death glare, Noah faced him. Dan pointedly refused to meet his gaze. "Noah was such a good sport. He wanted to do everything right for Elsie, and I knew her birthday was coming up. She'd told Noah she hated the spotlight so much, there was no way she wanted a birthday party. She wanted something nice and private, no one paying attention to her."

Noah's fists clenched in his lap.

Dan put an arm around Noah's shoulder, and Noah twisted away from him. Dan said to the entire table, "Elsie's best friend was Skye. I told Noah that Skye had said the birthday party was a test. If Noah really loved Elsie, he'd know she *did* want a birthday party. A big one, with the whole high school class, that way she'd have one last fling before leaving Brighthead. It was a safe way to get comfortable with people's attention before she went to college."

Noah raised his voice to project just as much as Dan's. "Except he was lying through his teeth."

Dan laughed. "Noah was good at planning heists, but not good at detecting them. On Elsie's birthday, he passed the test: he surprised her with a giant birthday party in his back yard, with the whole graduating class, plus the entire drama club, plus a bunch of folks from the regional vo-tech." He chucked Noah on the shoulder. "Great party, man."

Noah said, "It got ten times better once you invited the cops."

Dan sat back and raised his hands. "I had nothing to do with that."

"Nothing whatsoever to do with half of Brighthead being angry at me after they had to pick up their underage drinkers from the lockup because they brought their own booze?"

Dan said, "You weren't charged with anything, and neither was Elsie."

Noah struggled to keep his voice level. "And, if you recall, that stunt blew up our friendship."

Dan breezed it right off. "Nothing blew up. You went to college, and you never came home again."

Noah said to the friends across the table, "Because of him, Elsie dumped me."

Dan said, "She was a good sport at the party."

Noah flattened his tone. "Because she's an amazing woman. Afterward, she said I should have believed what she said, that she wasn't the kind of person who'd test you." Noah turned to Dan. "I didn't forget any of this."

Dan looked right at Noah. "After today, I'm well aware you haven't forgotten. But unlike Elsie, I *do* know how to take a joke."

Noah gestured at the table. "If you're talking about the strawberries, I can honestly say, I had nothing to do with that."

"And the hydrangea brace?"

"I have never heard of a hydrangea brace. But if you recall, Kevin here is dying for you to credit him with some awesome pranks, so if I were you, I'd turn my head to the right."

Kevin bowed his head and took the credit. How awesome for him, except Dan didn't give him a second look. "But you did break my social media passwords." Dan arched his eyebrows. "Mr. Cybersecurity Expert?"

Noah bit back a laugh. "You just affirmed for everyone present that you enjoy a good joke."

"I can, but look." He leaned in close, his tone abruptly serious. This wasn't a performance. "Don't mess with Skye. I can take a joke at my expense. I can deal with a strawberry cake. Oh, thanks," he said, turning to the server who'd just delivered a plate with a burger and fries. "I can deal with pointless errands and silly status updates. But do not mess with Skye."

Noah's eyes narrowed. "The way you didn't mess with Elsie? The way she didn't spend the evening of her birthday talking to a bunch of humorless police officers? For that matter, Skye herself was at that party and spent the evening talking to a bunch of humorless police officers."

"That was eight years ago, and we were all immature snots back then." He turned to Kevin. "Weren't we immature snots back in high school?" He turned back to Noah as though asking the question itself were the answer. "But not Skye. Skye's an amazing woman, and I don't want anyone hurting her. No bubblewrap under the carpet during the bridal march. No beehives in her bouquet. No exploding dye packs on her wedding gown."

Noah paused. "I never thought about bubble wrap under the bridal carpet. That's clever."

"Yeah, my dad did that for my uncle's third marriage. The bride loved it and ended up doing an impromptu dance down the aisle. The organist even changed the bridal march music to salsa."

Noah raised his eyebrows. "How good is Skye at salsa? Strawberry salsa?"

Dan's eyes were like steel. "I'm serious. Don't mess with her."

Noah raised his hands. "Fine. *Skye's the limit.* You, however? Watch your back."

Dan broke into a grin. "There's my man!"

Noah snorted. "Game on."

Dan fist-bumped him, then picked up his burger. "Darn right, it's game on."

Before he got even one bite, though, the background music halted, replaced immediately with a carnival fanfare. Dan's eyes flew open, and he pivoted toward the door.

A gigantic yellow duck bounded into the room, casting fistfuls of hard candy in every direction. It proceeded to a dais in front of the picture windows, and blew up a long blue balloon. "Greetings, everyone! I'm Stripes the Duck, and today, we're going to do magic tricks and balloon animals! Where's the guest of honor?"

Bellowing with laughter, Dan strode to the front. Noah pulled out his phone and started uploading live video to his social media.

"Usually the best man hires a stripper," he typed as the

video went live. "I guess Dan hired a Striper, which seems much better-geared to the relative maturity of the groom."

Within two minutes, Dan was wearing a balloon hat and holding a balloon doggie, and Stripes the Duck was pulling magic quarters from behind his ears.

Score: Noah and Elsie, 4. Dan: 0.

CHAPTER SEVEN

Elsie crossed her arms as Noah (gah, Szymczak,) slipped into the front seat of her car. She muttered, "Good job hiring a magical duck to make balloon animals. Dan looks to have enjoyed every single second of it."

The jerk didn't even blink about Elsie beginning a conversation as though he'd already been having it with her for twenty minutes. Instead, he handed her a cat made of balloons. "And?"

The balloons squeaked under her fingertips as she dutifully scritched the cat under its latex chin. "We're supposed to be getting payback, Szymczak. It's not payback if Dan had the most fun bachelor party that anyone in Brighthead can remember." She pulled away from the parking lot and glowered at the road. Dan's social media stream had been a flood of pictures of balloon animals—and some other balloon creations that she would have bet Stripes the Duck didn't normally make for toddler birthday parties. And which Stripes the Duck would probably deny under oath ever having made if confronted with the photographic evidence. "I should have known I could count on you to mess it up. It's like you never even listened to me."

"That's not fair. Half the humor in a prank comes from the way the person reacts. Dan happened to think it was hilarious and went right along with it."

Elsie muttered, "Then pick something he can't find hilarious."

"He was livid about the strawberries, but fortunately I could deny having anything to do with that." Noah frowned. "How did you change the menu?"

Elsie snickered. "The caterers called to confirm while Skye was in the shower. I chatted to them about what might be in season during late June."

Grinning, Noah said, "So...luck."

"Luck and quick thinking, if I do say so myself."

"You did say it yourself, so that at least is true. Hey!" He dodged as she tried to punch his arm. "Don't teach violence to the cat. The restaurant did serve Dan a hamburger and fries, at any rate. And a chocolate mousse pie."

"It was a given he wouldn't make it all the way to dessert." Elsie frowned. "Okay, but this just proves we need to plan better because we can't rely on luck or Skye leaving her phone unattended."

Noah said, "After tonight, Dan knows what I'm up to."

"Didn't take him long."

"You're still in the clear. He thought it was all me until Kevin tried to take credit, but Dan didn't look like he believed it."

Elsie chuckled. "Incursion?"

"Yeah, it's a word. I can also say things like *instantiate* if it makes you happy."

"Except it wouldn't."

"Then I can say it even more because I never stood a chance of making you happy in the first place," Szymczak said, and Elsie flinched. "Instantiation of a series of truly funny pranks will require a planning session."

Elsie pulled in at the Brighthead pier. "You make it sound like I stomp about the countryside, determined to wrestle the rubber bone of unhappiness from the clenched jaws of the Rottweiler of Joy."

Szymczak sat up. "And you thought *instantiate* was flowery language?"

"I'm actually not hard to make happy, thank you very much. I don't make a lot of demands, and say what I want."

"Yes, the way you said to Skye, 'I know you want your wedding in my beach house, but I'd prefer to see Dan lowered into a volcano, feet-first so I can hear him screaming longer.'"

Elsie glared at Szymczak. "Are you finished?"

"Have I started? You love to tell people you don't make demands, but you also don't tell them what you actually want—or what you don't want. Which does, in fact, make it impossible for us to make you happy."

She left the car and stalked onto the pier.

Summertime in Brighthead left Elsie swinging on a pendulum of emotions. The weather and the ocean and the character of the town made it so amazing. Bicycles and picnics and long walks on the rail trail. Horses—lots of horses. The tourism, however, bogged down the days, leaving them crowded and slow. She got shut out of her favorite places and couldn't park in her regular spots.

The last time she'd kissed Noah, it had been during the summer.

He followed her onto the pier. At this hour, most of the tourists were back in their rentals, but they were hardly alone. Elsie turned her back to Szymczak.

Her hair stood on end as he joined her at the railing. "You never wanted to see me again, and I respected that. You called me to come here and prank Dan. I came for you. Work with me. For planning purposes, what's the ultimate goal?"

"Payback."

"Clarify that, because breaking up him and Skye would hurt Skye. Also, he made me promise not to involve her in the pranks."

She frowned. "He did?"

"He loves her. Skye isn't at fault in anything Dan did, although maybe she's at fault for dating him."

"She says he's grown up."

"It's been a third of his life since graduation. He'd better have."

Szymczak had grown up, too. He articulated himself differently than he had back when they'd been dating. Back then, Elsie's biggest complaint had been that he wouldn't stand up to her. If she yelled at him for something, he retreated like a scolded puppy rather than defending himself. You'd think that would be a good thing, but it always left Elsie feeling adrift, like she could steer the two of them in the wrong direction and he'd know it, but he'd just let it happen. Of course, telling him he should be more assertive had immediately drawn the required compliance ("Okay, I'll be more assertive if you want,") followed by exactly no change in their dynamic.

He'd tended to evaporate before a stronger personality, and that was Dan. Szymczak couldn't match Elsie's energy in high school, and when he'd failed to defend her to Dan —failed even to listen to her when Dan said something opposite what she'd said—that had been the end. She needed a partner, not a minion.

Every time they'd talked about their future—a single future rather than these split futures they were living now —Elsie had fought a voice in the back of her head saying that Noah didn't know the real her. That he would never look out for her best interests because he barely even looked out for his own. Partners should stake out territory for one another. Partners should advocate for one another. Elsie didn't need to be a princess in a tower, but she wanted someone to ride to her rescue as often as she rode to his. He should know all these things. He should know to stand up for her sometimes. He said he loved her, so why didn't he know when she needed him to push back on her suggestions rather than just crumpling up like a tent when you pulled out the supports?

Partners shared authority. Minions did not.

Szymczak coming back to Brighthead when Elsie tugged the string had seemed like the Return of the Minion, except at some point in the last eight years, he'd learned to function on his own. Which, again, was good. As Szymczak himself had just said, high school graduation was a third of a lifetime ago for all of them.

Szymczak said, "Therefore, we need a goal. Do we want a series of pranks that leads to one crowning stunt, or do we want a bunch of random stuff that keeps Dan on his toes but has no predictable outcome?"

She said, "I want him to feel the way I felt."

Until those words emerged, softly and with the barest tremble, Elsie hadn't known what she was about to say.

Szymczak said, "And so I don't assume what you were feeling back then, what was it?"

He should know this. They'd broken up because she'd explained, over and over again, how she felt, and Szymczak never seemed to understand. Either that, or he'd understood but hadn't thought her feelings valid. Or maybe he'd thought her feelings valid but hadn't felt it worth the effort to make her comfortable.

At the end, she'd felt nothing but hopeless when she'd broken it off with Noah, and that's when the idiot had had asked for another chance. *This time,* he promised—this time he'd get it right if she'd just give him a chance.

She'd already given him fifty chances. She replied, "Goodbye is the end of the conversation, not the beginning of negotiations."

A week later, he'd driven off to college, and so had she, suffused with emptiness and betrayal and questions about why she hadn't been good enough for him to blossom into his best self for her. She'd toyed with the idea of starting things up when he returned next summer—except instead of returning to Brighthead with his mother, he'd gone to Portland to live with his father.

While the waves lapped the pier, Elsie swallowed hard. "I want Dan to feel humiliated. I want him to feel like everyone's against him."

After a minute, when Szymczak still hadn't replied, Elsie clenched her fists and stared directly down at water she could no longer see.

At last Szymczak cleared his throat. "Yeah. I can understand that." Another momentary silence. "Then we don't build up to something. Just pepper him with random pranks."

Elsie didn't raise her head.

He continued, "The wedding ceremony is off-limits, and so is Skye. The reception should still be fair game, so if we have a capstone prank, we do it then. But the rest of the time, we just, you know, make his life a series of jolting surprises."

As a planner, Szymczak sounded like he had in high school, and Elsie glanced at him. The pier lights left him oddly shadowed as he watched the lighthouse beam swing over the waves. He looked younger now than a moment ago—his facial features softer, his eyes hesitant. It was just like Noah from high school.

He *had* been timid then, hadn't he? In the past eight years, he'd picked up confidence Elsie didn't recognize. The Noah of her high school days had collapsed like a house of cards whenever Dan slapped his hand on the table. The Noah she'd invited to come prank her nemesis wasn't the Szymczak who'd arrived. The man at her side was a planner with an area of expertise and an understanding of strategy. He took charge when he should and backed off when backing off was appropriate.

Szymczak said, "Just so you know—I wasn't against you. I messed up royally by leaving you with that impression. You should have had an advocate in your corner, and I failed you."

She said, "That's water under the bridge."

"We're on a pier, and it's not water under the pier if we're still trying to get payback against a guy who barely remembers what he did. Although he still thinks it was hilariously funny." Szymczak clenched his fists. "He laughed, and I doubled what I wanted to do to him."

Elsie's nose wrinkled. "What more do you want to do?"

"Everything, now. I've set an alarm for two o'clock in the morning to post on his socials again, but I assume he expects that." He narrowed his eyes. "So—humiliated and alone. And, ideally, something that makes him think Skye doesn't love him."

Elsie straightened. "Hang on—"

"We can't hurt Skye. That doesn't mean she can't be involved." Szymczak faced Elsie. "Senior year, for Halloween, remember how we all went to school in costume? And who did we go as?"

Elsie gasped. "Oh!"

Szymczak had gone as rock star Edgar Chantz, and Elsie had gone as one of his backup singers. As drama club members, they hadn't won best theme costume because that kind of thing was just a popularity contest—but still, it looked darned good. Well, Noah had looked darned good. She'd made sure to fade behind his act like any good backup singer.

Szymczak prompted, "And is Skye still massively crushing on Edgar Chantz?"

"You mean, does she text me sobbing every time he releases a song and she hears it for the first time?" Elsie snorted. "You mean, does she still have a life-sized standee of Edgar Chantz in her bedroom at her parents' home?"

He laughed. "That opens up so many possibilities for your local small-town Edgar Chantz impersonator."

"It's better than that." Elsie bit her lip. "Guess whose song she really, really, really wanted for their first dance?"

His eyes flared. "Did Dan fight her on that?"

"You know, what if he happens to be a teensy bit jealous?"

Szymczak rubbed his chin. "It would be a shame if Edgar Chantz showed up at the wedding and objected to the marriage going forward."

Elsie laughed loud enough that she probably scared the fish, and she covered her face in her hands. "And you know what's even worse? I probably still have the costume!"

"No!"

"Yes! My mother never throws away a thing!" Elsie swiped tears from her eyes. "But not at the wedding."

"I know, I know. No bubble wrap under the bridal carpet, and no Edgar Chantz playing guitar and objecting to her marrying Dan when she could be marrying him."

She snickered. "So, step one is to climb into my mother's eaves and figure out where the Edgar Chantz gear ended up."

"No, step one is—" Szymczak stopped abruptly. "Step one is I apologize. Really apologize."

Elsie's breath caught.

"I didn't treat you well. You were right to break up with me, and I'm sorry. I didn't mean to make you feel like no one would advocate for you."

Elsie edged away from him. "Don't."

"The way you broke up with me, it changed the way I dealt with other people afterward. You told me, 'Goodbye isn't the start of negotiations,' and I had no idea what you meant. At least, not until I quit my first job because they were underpaying me and refused to raise my salary to industry standards. When I gave my two weeks' notice, and they offered a fifty percent pay raise on the spot. I shot back at them, 'Goodbye isn't the start of negotiations.' That's when I realized—all those ways I felt taken for granted in that job, all the ways I'd felt ignored and belittled, that's what I'd done to you."

Elsie closed her eyes.

"I was furious that it took the threat of ending the relationship for them to finally make the least effort to have me stick around. Except I couldn't stay angry at them because that's how I'd behaved toward you. All the frustration of dealing with them, that's what I put you through. At the time, I blamed you for not giving me a second chance, but what I didn't recognize was how you'd already given me a dozen chances, and I'd blown through every one of them without noticing."

Elsie swallowed hard. "It wasn't that bad."

"Then you're papering it over. When I've dated since then, I've monitored myself and diagnosed my own behavior to make sure I don't repeat the same mistakes. I've started looking at relationships the same way I look at internet security. Preventative maintenance, regular updates, intrusion detection, and watching for error codes that don't make sense."

Elsie forced a smile even though Noah wouldn't see it in the dark. "You must be the warmest heart in the room every Valentine's Day."

"It's even more amazing when I'm bootstrapping a relationship." He snickered. "All that to say, I did get my act together. I'm just sorry you had to suffer so I could have a learning experience."

"You keep using words like suffer." Elsie braced herself. "We were what, seventeen? If you'd already known everything about how to have a relationship, I'd kind of need to wonder what you'd been doing all along."

"It shouldn't take a PhD in psychology to know that when someone says, 'Don't do this,' you shouldn't do it. You were the best relationship I ever had, and yes, I wasn't mature enough to care for it properly." Noah snorted. "I'm sorry I listened to Dan. I'm sorry I ignored your consent. But if it's any consolation, I've also tried to change."

Change, so he could be a better man for someone else? Change, so some random person would reap the benefit of everything Elsie had gone through? No, thank you.

She said, "Have I changed?"

Szymczak turned toward her. "You're still full of mischief. You still don't want the spotlight. The revenge part is new and exciting. You've still got a loyal streak a mile wide if you're letting Skye use your beach house."

Elsie recoiled. "I wasn't full of mischief back then."

"Absolutely, you were. Dan still brags about filling up the vice principal's office with canned goods, but I remember whose idea that was."

Elsie raised her hands. "That wasn't mischief. It benefitted everyone."

"The prank having a good outcome doesn't mean it wasn't a brilliant prank *as well*." Szymczak chuckled. "But that's what I mean. I'd never have been able to come up with that. I'd have filled the vice principal's office with rudely-shaped balloons, only you immediately thought of a way to make it a positive. You were always bright and alive and thinking three steps ahead, and that was why I loved you."

As opposed to now, when she was dismal and half-dead and spending her life reacting to a stimulus six minutes after it happened?

He stopped abruptly, and Elsie backtracked—he'd just said he'd loved her back then, and he'd also said she hadn't changed. So...

No, he couldn't fall for her again. Not after so many tides had come in and out of this harbor, not after nearly a decade of anger and wondering why she'd never been good enough for him to become the man she'd needed him to be —except apparently, he'd gone ahead and become exactly that. Become it after she was no longer in the picture, but become it nevertheless.

He'd loved her then.

Did he love her now?

She didn't want him to. He was here for revenge, not to reopen a heart full of jagged pieces. She didn't even know whether he was dating anyone, although apparently at some point he had been. She wasn't dating anyone now— not for the past two years after she'd been aghast at Alan for leaving Skye at the altar, then at Skye for rebounding with Dan even though Skye knew how horrible Dan had been back in high school. Except the rebound never ended.

Love stopped you from seeing behind someone's mask. Or maybe it meant you did see behind the mask, but told yourself that they could change their face if you only loved them into beauty. If you loved your boyfriend into having a backbone, then he would stand up for you when you needed him to.

If love made one's judgment untrustworthy, how could someone justify letting herself fall in love? Ever?

That had been Elsie's question whenever she'd flirted with someone, whenever she'd gone out for coffee. How would she know if she was getting taken?

Noah hadn't deceived her. She'd known within a week that Noah had all the fortitude of a jellyfish, and in the back of her mind, she'd noted, "Someday, we're going to break up because he won't defend me." That wasn't even a case of hindsight being 20/20. Elsie written those exact words in her journal, and when she'd re-read that entry a year later, she'd immediately reached for a sticky note in her desk. "Listen to your instincts," she'd written to herself, and fixed it to the wall.

Her instincts had gone cold in the past eight years. They weren't telling her anything except that Noah was standing so close, and in the warm night, it would be easy for her skin to brush against his. She could stand nearer to him, and the ocean breeze would break around them both. She knew how he'd smell. She knew how softly he'd kiss, assuming he still kissed the same way. Tentative.

Except—hadn't his being tentative been the reason they broke up?

So instead of touching him, Elsie stood away from the railing. "Since you got that out of the way, our *next* first assignment will be hunting down the Edgar Chantz outfit in the attic."

Szymczak said, "Tomorrow morning?"

"They're going out for breakfast, so pop in around nine-thirty." Elsie rubbed her arms. "I'll drive you back to your car."

Szymczak trailed her as she walked along the

boardwalk. "Thanks. For the ride, and for hearing me out."

She hadn't accepted his apology. She hadn't said she'd forgiven him.

As she started the engine, she knew that without realizing it, in her heart, she'd done both.

She backed out of the space with a sigh. She needed to make sure her heart didn't go ahead and do anything else.

CHAPTER EIGHT

Noah arrived at the beach house only to have Elsie shoo him back out the door. "I don't want them to know you're here!"

He looked at the empty driveway. "They're not here to know what they don't know."

"If they come back! This is super-secret stuff." She giggled, her black hair tied in a ponytail. "You'll notice my car is gone, too."

She made him drive two blocks to a friend's driveway, and then they walked back. The sky was clear, the air sharp but not cold. Noah had forgotten how much he enjoyed summertime in Maine.

Just inside, he dropped his backpack on the couch. "No!" Elsie exclaimed as if he'd produced a gas can and a book of matches. "Secret! Think secret!"

"How much of a secret do I have to keep from people who aren't around?" Noah protested as she dragged him by the arm to her bedroom, which was not a place he'd intended to set foot. Fortunately he only had to set foot in there long enough to leave his backpack on her bed (not himself on her bed, which he was having increasing difficulty not thinking about the longer he stayed in Brighthead). He opened the bag up and produced a label-maker.

Elsie said, "And this is…?"

He worked the label maker until he came up with "doorknob." He peeled off the label and stuck it to her doorknob.

Her eyes widened. "Oh. My."

"They're going to know I was here." Noah snorted. "That was never in question."

In Dan's room, Noah generated labels with a gusto reserved for museum curators. "Bed." "Window." "Mirror." Elsie, by contrast, had an eye for the weird. On Dan's beach shoes, she printed out "flip" and "flop," one for each foot. While Noah affixed "toothbrush" to the appropriate item on the bathroom sink, Elsie was generating a label for "dirty glass."

She was absolutely brilliant, and that spark of mischief kept enticing him to watch over her shoulder while she worked. Her dark hair and quick eyes. Her slim fingers working the label-maker with a quickness that defied her recent introduction to the unit. "Bar of soap," she affixed to the soap in the bathroom, followed by Noah sticking "shower curtain" to the inside of that.

"Left sock," Elsie printed out, then unrolled a pair from the drawer, stuck the label inside a sock, and re-rolled the pair.

Ah, a time-bomb. Ideally, Dan should be finding these on his honeymoon, if not for weeks after getting home. And it was even more a time-bomb because Elsie did not then label "Right sock." Dan could just keep looking for that, maybe for months.

Noah tried to think like Elsie, and after that there were labels inside Dan's swim trunks, under the cap of his sunblock, and inside the travel case with his passport.

Elsie said, "Replacing his passport with a fake passport would be unduly cruel, so I'll constrain myself to thinking about it."

"That's the best part of a prank," Noah said, punching a dozen letters into a label. "Knowing you could have pulled it off, but you refrained because then you'd be worse than the person you're pranking."

He did, however, slap a label inside the suitcase. "Check your passport."

Elsie snorted. "Oh, that's evil."

"I didn't say I wasn't just as bad as Dan. Only that I don't want to be worse." He looked around. "Anything else?"

Elsie labeled a few things Dan had stuck in the fridge, but then she checked the time. "Let's go in the eaves. We still have a couple of hours, but I want to be good and gone before they return."

Noah nipped back into her bedroom to zip up the label maker. "It's kind of a shame we won't be here to see the reaction."

"The sacrifices you'll make in the pursuit of vengeance." She grinned. "Let's go."

Except she didn't leave her room. Of all things, she went to one of the set-in bookshelves and started working it out of the wall.

He got up beside her. "Do you have a secret passageway?"

"This is how you get into the eaves."

Now that he knew it was there, Noah realized the outline around the set-in bookshelves was, in fact, a slot. He got alongside Elsie. "Let me help."

Her arm brushed by his, sending a thrill up his body. She said, "It comes straight back, but it's difficult because of the carpet."

He focused on working the bookshelf backward rather than thinking about her right beside him. It wasn't easy. There wasn't much to occupy his brain, and therefore his brain kept suggesting moving sideways and touching her.

Instead he should think about her taking any one of these books and clocking him over the head, since there was no way she would consent to even one of the things he was thinking about. He choked out, "If you let go, I'll walk it back a bit at a time."

In an awful moment, she did step away from him, but at least he could avoid his impulses. The bookshelf moved awkwardly, although not as awkward as Noah felt right now, and then Elsie said, "That's enough."

She slipped into the eaves, and a light flared on. "Come on."

He lit the flashlight on his phone, and then slipped in behind her.

It was hot back here. "Hang on," she said, and to his horror, Elsie gripped her hoodie and slipped it up from her waist, over her shoulders and head, and then shook herself free of its confines. That did nothing whatsoever to relieve the heat in Noah's body, so he pulled off his own hoodie and left it on top of hers. Their leftover body heat would mingle. Noah would just...well, suffer.

In a crawl, Elsie led Noah through the storage area where her mother had, as promised, saved everything anyone ever had in the entire town of Brighthead. Noah got a good look at Elsie's hips and legs as she moved. *She's getting revenge on me, too.* This much was obvious. Giving him a good look at everything he'd never touch again was the best prank ever. If anything, maybe she and Dan had organized this between them.

Noah grinned. Maybe Elsie was a double-agent. She could set up Noah to get revenge on Dan while simultaneously setting things up to make Noah eat his heart out.

She sat up in an alcove and hooked the portable lantern from beam. "This seems like high-school era stuff."

The alcove was slanted and stuffy, not yet roasting in the day's sunlight but veering that way. Mrs. Jenner had shoved boxes as far under the eaves as she could go, leaving aisles to access the boxes closest to the roof's edge. Elsie edged forward on her knees. "Oh, yearbooks!"

With a groan, Noah said, "Do we have to?"

"But there's that picture of you and Dan climbing that tree at the student government picnic." She snickered. "How can you turn that down?"

"Because there's also the picture of you and me at prom, and I thought you wanted to forget about that." She couldn't argue with this logic, could she?

"I never forgot that. You looked awesome in that tux."

Ah, she *could* argue with it. "I had to match your awesomeness in that raspberry gown and those silver heels."

She glanced at him. "You remember?"

"One of us needed to remember." She'd looked amazing. She looked amazing all the time, but that night, she'd been poured into that gown and had her hair piled atop her head. Nowadays she wore her hair shorter, but her body was just as lithe. When she moved, she had confidence, as if she'd gotten used to what her body could do.

Except he shouldn't be thinking about her body. Noah shifted uncomfortably. "Keep going. If we've excavated to the senior year of high school, the costumes should be a little behind the yearbook boxes."

"And the after-party," Elsie said while she moved further into the eaves. "Where we just sat out on the rocks by the water while everyone else watched horror movies."

The characters in horror movies never predict the ruin that's about to unfold. Noah hadn't predicted it back then, either. He and Elsie had talked away the night under the stars, the wind lifting a few strands of hair that had escaped her updo. They'd sat on the rocks planning how they were going to make long distance work for them. Elsie was drawing up a schedule of how often they could talk and text, that way they'd have freedom to make friends and live the full college experience, but they could keep in touch with each other. Noah had wanted to go with the flow, but Elsie had been so nervous. Nervous about losing him. As long as she knew when he'd call, she'd promised, she could survive the times in between without worrying.

Losing him was the worst thing she could imagine happening that night. Six weeks later, she was going to go ahead and lose him.

Noah said, "That was a good night, but the rocks weren't exactly comfortable."

He'd draped his tuxedo jacket around her shoulders because she was cold, but neither one wanted to return inside to the dramatic music and the artificial buttery smell of popcorn.

When Elsie didn't respond, Noah added, "It's not comfortable up here, either."

"Yeah." She got onto her belly and wiggled under the narrowest part of the eaves, the floor creaking beneath her. "Crud. I think this is the box, but it's wedged under."

Noah aimed his flashlight at a box dutifully marked with, "Costumes." "You want me to pull it out?"

"I think I can get it."

Lying along the floor, she had no leverage. Noah got closer, then lay out next to her. "You get your arm around the back, and I'll pull on this corner while you push."

They tried, but although the board groaned beneath him, Noah couldn't get enough of a grip. "You back out and I'll give it a shot."

The creaking board signaled Elsie's attempt to wiggle backward out of the aisle—but then a door slammed below them.

Both of them froze in position.

"Dan?" Elsie whispered, as though Noah had any better idea than she had.

Another door opened and shut, followed by a muffled voice that sounded like Skye's. Then a response in Dan's register.

Noah whispered, "You said they had a whole day planned."

Elsie breathed back, "They did."

She started edging backward, but the board groaned,

and Skye's voice filtered up. "What was that?"

Noah put a hand on Elsie. "Stay put," he hissed.

"How long are they going to be in the house?"

He stretched his neck to put his mouth close to her ear. "If we can hear them through the vent, assume they can hear us."

Elsie's muscles relaxed under his touch, but Noah couldn't make it happen, not even to stay still.

Skye's laughter broke through, and Noah grinned. Elsie giggled, keeping it soft. "Found one," she whispered.

The voices got louder and softer as Dan and Skye moved nearer or further from the ducts. Skye kept announcing words they'd printed on the labels. "Mirror!" "Ocean view!" Skye was having a blast. Dan's laughter came through, too, although his voice was less distinct. "Dirty glass," he exclaimed from the bathroom, where the acoustics traveled especially well to the attic.

Noah murmured, "That was yours."

Elsie snickered. Gosh, she was close.

"Toilet. Hot water. Cold water. Soap." A pause. "Toothpaste. Toothbrush." They must be in the medicine cabinet now. "Shelf. These are awesome."

Nearly glowing, Noah wished he could see the expression on Dan and Skye's faces, but he could hear in their voices how they were smiling. To Elsie, he whispered, "You did great."

Elsie whispered back, "Don't I know it?"

It got even warmer in the attic, and not just because of the sun baking the roof.

Skye said, "You think this was Noah? I thought Noah can't get in here."

"Unless you think Elsie's doing this."

A long silence. This had, in fact, been part of Noah's plan: making them laugh, and also sending a clear message that Noah could touch all their stuff.

Meanwhile, also protecting Elsie, because that silence meant Skye didn't think Elsie was responsible.

Dan sounded dismissive. "Right now I'm thinking Noah

could march into the US Mint with twelve dudes he broke out of Rikers Island and then waltz out again with each one carrying a full sack on his shoulders." He snorted. "I told you, he came to Brighthead just to mess with us."

Skye said, "Should we tell him to leave? I mean, it would cause problems, but we could disinvite him."

"Even if we disinvite him, he's in Brighthead. He's going to do whatever he wants." Dan's voice was a lot more cheerful than his words. "I wouldn't worry. Noah promised he wouldn't mess with the ceremony, and no matter how much he's changed, his personality seems the same. He won't break a promise."

Beside Noah, Elsie tensed. Of course, in her mind, he'd broken a promise. With the very best and most honorable of intensions, he'd broken his word to her and would never again be trustworthy.

From Skye: "It could have been Kevin. You said it was my phone that sent the text about the hydrangeas, but how would Noah have gotten my phone?"

"The same way he's breaking my passwords. He's a computer geek." Dan's words had gotten clearer. When Noah attempted to recreate the floorplan in his mind, he thought Dan's bedroom might be below them, and now the bride and groom might be standing directly beneath the register.

Gosh, Elsie was so close. He edged back, but the board creaked. Skye said, "That sound, again."

"It's the wind. We're right on the beach." Silence from Dan for a moment. "Look, no harm done. So far, it's been a bunch of annoyances."

"He tried to ruin your bachelor party!"

"He didn't ruin my bachelor party. If anything, Kevin is probably planning on having Stripes the Duck deliver his proposal to Jen."

Skye sighed. "I don't know why Elsie even made me invite him."

Dan said, "Because Noah adored her? And maybe she wanted to start things up with him again?"

Noah fought the thrill that threatened to engulf him. Realistically, Elsie had planned no such thing—he knew that, now and forever. She'd found her backbone, and she'd found her balance, and having everything she needed in her life, there was no room for a former messed-up boyfriend.

She wanted a partner in crime, not a partner.

But still, he could hope.

Elsie shifted her weight slowly, carefully, to more easily balance herself. This left her on her side, facing Noah. Her breath danced over his throat.

Skye said, "Not the way she talks about him. Do you think he looked like he wanted to get back with her?"

"Noah just wants to get back *at me*." Dan laughed. "It really is just a bunch of annoyances so far. I've always loved a good prank, and frankly, his pranks so far aren't even good ones."

Noah bristled. Elsie raised a hand and put her finger on his lips.

Warmth flooded through him. She breathed, "Not a word."

Not a word. Instead, he kissed her fingertip.

Elsie stiffened, but Noah kissed her palm, then angled his head and kissed her wrist.

He shouldn't be doing this. And yet, she wasn't recoiling. She could have swiveled her wrist and grabbed his throat. She could have pushed his face away. Instead, she let him keep tracing his lips along the small bone of her wrist, then around to the back of her hand.

Skye said, "What would be a good prank?"

Noah didn't listen to the answer. He lowered Elsie's arm and stretched forward to kiss her mouth. Her lips softened, and she kissed him back.

Heat flooded him. Not just the stuffy heat of an attic under the rising sun. Air barely moved as the attic breathed, but against him, Elsie breathed and kissed him again. He couldn't pull her closer because the board would creak, and then Dan might go searching for the source of the sound. But, oh, they were together, and Noah had longed for this ever since the moment Elsie had stepped into his rented room and he'd remembered the way she moved and the sound of her voice and her every expression.

She nibbled his lip, then kissed his chin, and then he flexed his neck so she could kiss his throat. He took a chance and rested his hand on her waist, but he didn't dare tug her close. Not with Dan and Skye talking beneath them. He hooked his fingers into her belt loops, then turned his face toward hers so she could kiss his mouth again.

Sweat stung his eyes. Her body heat felt like a live volcano before him, and all he wanted was to turn the heat up higher, pull her on top of him and lose himself in the miasma of attic air and frustrated longing.

A door slammed, and the vibrations shot through the board beneath him.

Silence. Then, more silence.

Elsie was breathing hard. After a fully silent minute, Noah put his hand on her shoulder, but she moved away, saying, "I think they're gone."

Absolutely, the worst prank of all was going to be this—making him want what he could never have again. Except Elsie had wanted that, too, hadn't she? Or was it all a game? Had she arranged for Dan to trap them in the attic so Noah would get a little too excited?

Could he pull her back to him and kiss her again? Would she allow him to run his lips from her ear down her jaw line and then back to her lips again?

Because he'd allow that. If she let him, he'd be all for that. Enthusiastically.

Elsie took matters into her own hands by worming her way backward on her stomach, dragging the box.

Noah let the box get past and then followed her, also working backward while lying prone. When they could finally sit up, they worked open the box to see what was on top, but he thought Elsie's hands were shaking.

"Looks like the right one." His voice wasn't any steadier than her fingers. "We're good to go."

When they got back to the bookcase, she shouldered against it to escape the humid eaves, and they both spilled back into air cool enough to raise prickles on Noah's sweaty skin.

Her bedroom door was shut. He worked the bookcase back into the wall, then gave it a final push until it stood flush again. And speaking of flushed, across the room, Elsie's skin was red from the heat. Or from embarrassment.

Noah ventured, "Should I apologize for that?"

Elsie forced a smile. "I'd feel like a hypocrite if I accepted it, so– no."

Radar on, he joined her at the box, but she started laying folded costume pieces between them. As she reached again into the box, he rested a hand on hers, and she stopped moving.

He said, "I'd be lying, too, so—"

Still not looking at him, she said, "So don't apologize."

He squeezed her hand. "What if we upped the difficulty level on the pranking?"

Puzzled, she met his eyes.

"What if the best prank of all would be not letting Dan win?" He edged toward her. "What if we defeated Dan by undoing the breakup he caused?"

She shook her head. "This is— I don't know what I'm feeling."

He tilted his head. "You thought you knew five minutes ago."

"No. I thought I knew three days ago, but then you turned up, and now I don't know anything anymore."

Noah said, "You thought you hated me?"

"With flames and smoke coming out of my ears, absolutely." She turned away. "You can't sway me by being so darned cute, Szymczak. You're smart and cunning and you've got those eyes, and then you say things that make me think you adore me, and then I have no idea what to do."

Noah said, "What if I do adore you?"

"What if I think you adored me back then, only you had the spine of a jellyfish?"

Noah said, "What if eight years turned me into a vertebrate?"

She snorted. "And what if you still make me laugh?"

He reached for her shoulder. "What if you gave me another chance?"

Helpless, she turned her face to him, and then he was kissing her again, this time where he could breathe and move and put his hands on her, and she melted against him. Her mouth, on his. The sweat still hadn't evaporated off both of them, but he didn't care. He wanted her in his arms, all of her, her damp hair and her urgent mouth and her closed eyes. He wanted her near, and for now he had everything he wanted.

CHAPTER NINE

This was not going as intended.

Not even the pranks were going as intended. Dan was loving every one of them. Dan, Dan the jerk, seemed to love having his food turned into strawberries and his social media turned into a scandal rag. Dan was strutting around Brighthead wearing his balloon animal hat, and Elsie was slouching around Brighthead in a fug of confusion, wearing the taste of Noah on her mouth.

They'd abandoned the house. They'd gone for coffee because a public location would keep them out of one another's arms. They needed clear heads, and the two of them alone in a house—alone in her bedroom, for pity's sake—was the opposite of clearing their heads.

While Elsie sat at a table in the back, coiled tighter than a clock spring, Noah ordered their coffees at the counter. Blast, but she had no self control around him. It had been difficult enough pulling away from him in the attic where the air was a hundred five degrees. Once they were back downstairs and he'd come onto her like that? Her resolve melted faster than an ice cube on the pavement.

Worse, she couldn't keep thinking of him as Szymczak now. In her head, he'd pirouetted right back into "Noah" status, and everything about him felt just so comfortable. It seemed right for him to know what kind of coffee she'd choose even though it had been eight years and he'd never set foot in this six-year-old coffee shop. She hadn't bothered offering him money for the coffee, although now she regretted that, because it felt natural when he predicted her order to just say, "Sure, and I'll grab a table."

Elsie tried to roll out her shoulders. No use. They were tight like the cables on a suspension bridge, and everything was wrong in the best way. Or right in the worst way.

Noah approached with two coffees and a paper plate with a gigantic cinnamon roll, topped with melting butter. Heaven help her. He might as well be holding a spear and saying, "I know all your weak points."

He also held two knives and two forks. "Let's go halfsies."

She drew her coffee closer. "You're a grown man, and you said halfsies?"

"There are words grown men are forbidden to say?"

"They updated the list last year, dork." She didn't look at him as she cut the cinnamon roll in *halfsies* for His Majesty. "Halfsies is a new addition, along with 'edgelord' and cutesy.'"

"Bummer." He lobbed a triangle off the cinnamon roll with the side of his fork. "Should I start submitting all my speeches to you ahead of time for approval?"

She raised her eyebrows. "I shouldn't have said anything and let you go down in flames during your next job interview."

"Fortunately, all my lunchtime job interviews have involved the executives each ordering for themselves. I've never had to go halfsies on a meatball with the hiring manager."

Elsie sipped her coffee, and it was doctored up perfectly. Maybe she should have changed her coffee-drinking in the last eight years so she could have sneered, "It's no longer two sugars. I've moved *on*, Szymczak!"

I thought I'd moved on. Her throat tightened. *I've lived eight years without him, and I was prepared to live another eighty years without him. How could a few days invert all my expectations?*

Noah looked around as he drank his coffee. He, apparently, had changed: he was taking his coffee black. "If this place had existed when I was in high school, I'd never have left."

"You'd have gotten a job here and won employee of the month for fifteen consecutive months by looking customers dead in the eye and upselling them with whatever they secretly wanted to buy."

Noah flinched. "You sound angry. Am I upselling you?"

Again she looked at him, but this time to gauge his actual feelings. *Mortified*, she decided.

For all that Noah didn't give a care about Dan's anger, her apparent anger was hurting him.

He shouldn't be caring for her. All along, she'd been guarding her heart against caring for him now that he was back—since she like an idiot had invited him back—and not once had she planned for what would happen if he'd never entirely let go of her. The breakup had been her idea, but in eight years, Noah would have moved on. She'd moved on. She'd dated and had her heart broken and stood beside Skye during a heartbreak.

"My life is fine without you," she said as though she'd been saying all that out loud. "A few years ago, I was at my job and I realized, I can do this forever. I don't need a guy in my life. I had a first date that night with someone new, and I thought, I don't have to start this over again."

Noah's eyes lowered. "You don't need anyone. You're doing fine. You look great."

"I know," she added, although that sounded proud. But

she was proud of everything she'd made for herself, so she didn't walk it back. "I don't have to settle for anything or anyone. Everything's okay. Skye got her heart shattered about the same time I made that decision, and seeing her so desperate afterward—desperate enough to date Dan—it was just horrifying. I don't have to do that to myself."

Noah said, "Which is, when you think about it, the best possible compliment you can give any guy you do stay with. Do you think guys enjoy looking at a woman and thinking, 'She only stays with me because she's helpless'? I wouldn't want a partner who *couldn't* walk away. That's the fastest possible trip to buyer's remorse."

Elsie glanced out the window. From here, it was impossible to see the ocean, but in Brighthead, you never really forgot it was there. It was in the wind and the salt and the way the trees bent westward, away from the relentless breeze. "You're more confident than you were in high school."

Noah said, "Aren't we all?"

"Skye isn't." She sighed. "I am. You are. Dan never suffered from a lack of confidence in the first place, and half the guys in the bridal party are cut from the same cloth." She smirked. "Speaking of cut from the same cloth, I accidentally changed the wedding colors with the tuxedo place."

"You are brilliant." Noah forked off a bit more of the cinnamon roll. "I mean that. I'm not sorry I kissed you in the attic, and I'm not sorry we kissed again afterward." As heat crawled up her cheeks, he continued, "Also, I wouldn't be sorry about kissing you again. But that's what we're here to talk about."

She got a forkful of cinnamon roll for herself to delay answering—to force a silence so uncomfortable that Noah would have to keep talking and maybe say something so offensive that she could tell him, "Leave me alone, you pig." Except he dwelled in the silence while she chewed and swallowed, and in that silent moment, he seemed entirely comfortable waiting for her consent. He wasn't reaching for her hand or eyeing her body nor even staring at her face in the hopes of bending her to his will.

If you'd respected me like this in high school, we'd be celebrating our fourth anniversary right now. She swallowed and chased it with a gulp of coffee. *Our daughter would be Skye's flower girl, and I'd be pregnant with your son, and you'd be with Dan getting fitted for your tuxedo and laughing about the orange bow ties.*

Her eyes stung, and she grabbed a paper napkin to blot them so she wouldn't look like a canned soup commercial.

Noah slumped backward. "Blast."

"I hate you." She pressed the napkin into her face. "You're supposed to be a monster."

Noah averted his eyes. "I'm not even good at that."

She leaned her face hard into her palms.

His voice was tentative. "I guess that's a no for kissing you again."

He was trying to make her smile, and it was awful because he was being cute and sweet and it was just like the Noah she remembered. And the Noah she remembered had broken her heart.

Except—the Noah she remembered had also had the moral fortitude of a kite in a whirlwind. The Szymczak in front of her had a backbone. He wanted her. He wanted her to want him.

And he was letting the latter persona dictate his actions, rather than the former.

He'd grown. He'd changed. And she...

She crumpled the napkin in one hand and reached for him with the other. He flipped his hand over, and they were clasping hands across the table. They hadn't done that for eight years.

Her voice was a whisper. "You can't let me down again. If I say yes— If I give you another chance, you can't let me down."

Noah sounded urgent. "I don't want to let you down."

"You have to promise you'll listen to me. You won't let anyone jerk you around."

Noah's mouth twisted into a half-smile. "Well, you're jerking me around. If I'm not letting anyone—"

"Stop." She bit her lip. "About me, you listen to me. About you, you do what you want. I can't let you break my heart again. I promise to be honest with you if you promise to believe the things I say."

Last time, she'd entrusted him with everything about herself. She'd fallen hard and held back nothing. She'd told him her dreams and her fears and her pain, and when Dan tricked Noah into believing she was lying, Noah had acted as if all her inner workings were nothing.

Being with him now meant being once again with someone who knew—who already knew—all the awkward and damaged pieces of her. Not the details of the last eight years, but the details of her heart. That was dangerous. He hadn't proven trustworthy with those details before.

Noah squeezed her hand. "I can't prove myself trustworthy if you don't trust me first."

She said, "One strike, and you're out."

"That's more than fair." He took a deep breath. "In return, be clear with me. Don't expect me to read your mind, and never tell yourself that if I really cared about you, then I would know what you want."

Elsie's brows contracted. "I never did that."

Noah looked at her patiently.

"I only did that a few times." She glanced aside. "And only about things you should have known about, like when I told you to pick an ice cream flavor for me, and you came back with vanilla even though you knew what kinds of flavors I liked."

Noah said, "That's exactly what I mean. If you promise that I won't have to guess what you want, then I won't *second-guess* what you said."

She met his eyes, and her throat tightened. He looked sincere. He wanted a second chance. He was still all those things he'd been before the day he'd broken her heart, and he was promising not to break it again.

She squeezed his hand. "Okay. We take it slow. You get

only one shot."

He leaned in. "And do I get only one kiss?"

She leaned over the table toward him. "Maybe more than one," then closed her eyes as he kissed her again.

CHAPTER TEN

He had a chance.

They drove back to his rental unit in convoy to prepare the next prank, but this was the only thought repeating in Noah's head: he had a chance.

At some point, Noah would have to re-negotiate that "one chance" stipulation, because he knew himself. If he wanted to be with Elsie for a lifetime, at some point he was going to muck things up. Any guy would muck things up given time, but knowing who he was—not to mention their past and their baggage—Noah figured for himself it was a certitude.

Also, Elsie didn't have the best history of being clear about what she wanted. How could he prove to an angry woman who hadn't said what she meant that she hadn't actually said it…? Not going to happen.

So yeah, the key would have to be laying down enough trustworthiness that when Noah finally blew it, at least

Elsie could say, "You probably meant to get it right," and give him the benefit of the doubt. Which would be...what? Three months? Three years?

Noah made sure not to run any stop signs or open his car door into the side of Elsie's sedan. That would bring the measure to three minutes—hardly enough time to generate good will.

Elsie shook her head. "This rental..."

He hissed a hush at her, then gestured to the open windows in the main house. Elsie giggled. Noah said, "It has a bed and a shower and a toilet—and an oven. Which is what we really needed."

The beach house had an oven, too, but it also had Dan and Skye.

While Elsie preheated the oven, Noah checked Dan's social media, where Dan still hadn't noticed the childhood photos Noah had so generously posted on his behalf. That might be, just possibly, because Noah had blocked Skye from seeing Dan's posts and then turned off all Dan's notifications. The photos were accumulating many, many comments.

Elsie picked up the boxes of cake mix on the table. "I'm still not sure how this is going to work."

"But you trust me, right?"

She hesitated. "Well, more like, I believe this can't go fantastically wrong."

"Fair enough." Noah opened all the windows because he could already tell the whole apartment was about to turn into an oven. "But we agree at the very least that this venture meets the ever-growing criteria for fair game."

These were the current stipulations:

1) No hurting Skye.

2) No disrupting the ceremony.

3) Nothing incriminating Elsie.

4) Following all Elsie's stipulations on everything.

5) No costing Skye and Dan any extra money.

6) Dialing up the annoyance factor so Dan didn't keep enjoying the pranks and maybe got a little paranoid.

In effect, this was a heist movie where the heroic team needed to crack a safe at the end of a hallway criss-crossed by laser tripwires, so the team acrobat would need to limbo under some of them, vault over others, and swivel like a gymnast to get past the last. All while the alarms were screaming and the authorities were pounding up the stairwell.

In a way, that made it more fun. By the day of the wedding, Dan ought to be jumping out of his skin with nerves and trusting nothing at all. Which, really, was how Noah should have responded eight years ago when Dan told him Elsie was testing him over a birthday party.

As of this morning, all Dan and Skye's vendors were locked down. Noah had already called the florist, and when he hadn't been able to give the password, the florist had hung up on him.

That was a shame, because he'd been about to give Skye's flowers a massive upgrade. If she were going to throw the bouquet Noah had planned, she'd have needed a trebuchet.

That reminded him. "Did Skye text you about the tuxedo fitting?"

Elsie giggled. "Do you think Dan looks terrific in orange?"

Noah snorted. "He probably does, the monster. He looks good in everything."

Elsie teased, "Do you think he'll look good in green?"

"You mean, with envy during tonight's welcome party?" Noah grinned. "Let's find out."

Noah had never heard of a "welcome party" before this week, but immediately on hearing about it, he'd welcomed yet another occasion to put Dan Bluett in the hot seat.

Apparently it wasn't enough to have an engagement party, a bridal shower, a bridesmaid luncheon, a bachelor and bachelorette party, a rehearsal dinner, and a wedding reception. With lots of family members traveling from out of town, it was also incumbent on the with-it bride and groom to host a welcome party two days before the wedding, for everyone who'd traveled in. But this was low key: they'd rented the Oddfellows Hall and set up an online signup sheet to bring food.

It was too bad Dan didn't know he'd volunteered to bring the dessert.

A spectacular, memorable dessert.

A spectacular, memorable dessert that Skye didn't know about because like a good Maid of Honor, Elsie had kept telling her that she would take care of all the potluck details, so the bridal couple wouldn't have to.

In the cramped basement rental, Noah assembled two boxes of yellow cake mix while Elsie greased two large baking pans.

"The listing said complete kitchen," he muttered. "There aren't measuring cups."

"You don't need a measuring cup to make a box cake mix." Elsie cocked her head. "Why would you?"

"You have to add oil and water."

She started opening drawers. "Ta-dah!"

"That's dry measure."

"It's exactly the same."

He frowned. "It's not. I've always been told it's not the same."

She arched her eyebrows. "Everyone lied. They're entirely the same."

He ignored her and kept looking in drawers, but yeah, no liquid measure. Meanwhile she poured the oil into the dry cup and eyeballed the halfway mark.

"This is no way to conduct science," he muttered.

"I'm not trying to conduct science. I'm trying to make a cake."

Except, for this prank to work, the cake had to be good. Elsie eyeballed the water levels, and then she whisked the cake mix together.

Elsie said, "This had better be truly disgusting when we're done."

"Vile," promised Noah.

This had been one of the first plans Noah had come up

with, only he couldn't figure out how to fly up with it already assembled. Ergo, needing a room with a kitchen. And needing time for a grocery run. And the hope (which bore fruit) that no one would recognize him as he loaded the checkout belt with cake mix, sandwich cookies, pudding...and a brand new cat litter pan.

The idea wasn't his own. Last year, Noah's office-mates had held a Gross-Out Party, featuring all manner of tasty foods prepared to look disgusting. He'd arrived to a buffet loaded with cookies that looked like puppy chow, pigs-in-blankets resembling swollen fingers with dark red fingernails, mini marshmallows dabbed in peanut butter and stuck on toothpicks (served out of a cotton swab box!) and eyeballs on a stick that turned out to be cake pops. The crowning glory of that event had been the pineapple punch served in a brand new toilet bowl, but what would work best as a wedding prank was the Kitty Litter Cake.

Noah used the apartment's blender to start crumbling two entire pounds of sandwich cookies. If the homeowners were upstairs, they must wonder whether their house were about to be cordoned off as a crime scene.

Before Noah knew it, he was grinding up cookies with Elsie's arms around his waist and her cheek resting against his shoulder. He swallowed hard. "Keep doing that and I won't be safe to operate heavy machinery."

"The welcome party isn't until six o'clock." Elsie walked her fingers up his chest. "We've got time."

He swallowed hard. "Sure about that, are you?" As she giggled, he said, "If I mess this up because you're being mischievous, I'm totally telling Skye on you."

"What would you tell her?"

"I'd tell her about this." He turned away from the blender and put his hands on Elsie's cheeks, then guided her lips toward his.

Which was exactly when someone knocked on the door.

Elsie stifled a laugh. "It's Grandma Jenner!"

Sighing, Noah kissed her quickly, then opened up to find the homeowner holding a liquid measuring cup. "You needed this?"

There weren't enough confused exclamations in the universe to express anything Noah felt at that moment, although, "Oh, for crying in a rusty bucket!" might have come closest, so all he said was, "Thank you."

The homeowner then entered the premises, which probably violated every one of the vacation share's regulations, and said, "Elsie Jenner? I thought I heard your voice! How have you been?"

Elsie blurted out, "Mrs. Edgemont?"

Elsie's grandmother should rest assured: to this very day, Elsie was very well-protected. It was kind of a wonder that when they were side by side in the eaves, Noah's second grade baseball coach hadn't banged on the roof, calling, "I noticed some leaves in your gutters, so I'm here to check the soffit vents!"

(Did that even make sense? Living in an apartment, Noah never needed to deal with anything like that. But surely someone dealt with gutters and soffit vents, and the way the universe was unfolding, shouldn't it have happened right then?)

Mrs. Edgemont was delighted to catch up with Elsie, so the two of them made properly-measured pudding together with long pauses for noise while Noah finished grinding cookies. In the times between grinding sessions, he learned Mrs. Edgemont had been Elsie's scout leader for five years.

Noah stirred drops of green food coloring into the cookies until he had greenish-yellow gravel.

Now would have been a good time to continue flirting and kissing, except like a good scoutmaster, Mrs. Edgemont was on guard to protect Elsie's virtue with catch-up conversation. How was Mrs. Jenner? Oh, she'd moved away from Brighthead? What was she doing now?

Noah said, "Elsie does therapy with hippos."

Elsie blew at her hair. "Seriously, Noah?"

The timer went off, so Noah had to pull the cakes from the oven, and that meant Elsie couldn't kill him right there.

"It's hippotherapy," she said. "Horses. Not hippos."

His life spared, Noah went to work softening chocolate taffies in the microwave while Elsie gave Mrs. Edgemont a rundown on what exactly was hippotherapy and how no, she wasn't working with hippos. Which, given how her explanation to Mrs. Edgemont was word-for-word the same explanation she'd given Noah, she must have to clarify on a regular basis.

More kissing was, it seemed, out of the question, so Noah focused his annoyance on the now-softened chocolate taffies, which he shaped into as many disgusting rounded pieces as he could.

This was such a small town. Of course he would have ended up renting a room from Elsie's former scout troop leader.

Elsie said, "Do you need any help?"

Standing before a plate that looked like a pile of cat by-products, he waved her off. Besides, it was interesting to hear Elsie talking to his nosy landlady-for-five-days. As she talked, she got more into the details of hippotherapy, and talked more about her clients. She couldn't name them, of course, but he heard about little kids who only ever spoke around the horses. He heard about a woman who'd broken both hips in a ski accident who needed a lift to lower her onto the horse, but who came three times a week because horse therapy was the only way she'd ever walk again.

Elsie saw damage in the world and extended a hand to heal it. The focus of the therapy was the horse—but in a way, the credit also went to the handler. Elsie was the one walking the horse and keeping the horse calm. Elsie was the one gentling a frightened child until the child could stay still for the therapy to take place. Elsie, who never wanted the spotlight, had managed to stay out of the spotlight even when everything good was happening because of her.

He glanced across the kitchen. Her eyes were bright, her words quick, her gestures measured. He went warm.

She caught his eye. "Yes?"

"Oh, nothing." Instead, Noah got the dish soap to wash the brand new cat pan, then the cat litter scoop. He fitted the pan with a plastic liner, then glanced again at Mrs. Edgemont, who had no intention of leaving.

Elsie said, "Oh, this is going to be the fun part. Come help!"

Praying Mrs. Edgemont had a sense of humor, Noah stepped back. They broke up the sheet cakes into bits while he mixed the pudding with half the cookie crumbs. He mixed it in with the cake, and it already looked gross.

Mrs. Edgemont ventured, "You said this is for Skye? Aren't you two still friends?"

Elsie said, "Oh, trust me, it'll be hilarious."

Noah poured the remainder of the crumbs over the top of the cake to create a lovely cat litter effect, then handed the plate to Elsie. "Are you ready for the final touches?"

Her nose wrinkled. "I don't want to touch those at all."

As Mrs. Edgemont took the plate, one corner of her mouth quirked up. "Why, I do believe I'd love to."

In a minute, she had a realistic smattering of cat doots embedded in the cake, including one last piece she smashed into the edge of the cat pan. "I've owned cats for forty years," she reassured Elsie. "This is perfectly nauseating."

Noah worked the kitty litter scoop into the cake. "I think they'll love it."

Mrs. Edgemont said, "As long as you don't get in trouble for this."

"Why would I?" Elsie asked. "The groom is the one on the signup sheet as providing dessert."

"Oh, dear." Mrs. Edgemont hesitated. "Don't bring it to the hall just yet."

Two minutes later, she was back downstairs with a cardboard box large enough to fit the entire cat pan. They boxed up the cake while Elsie wrote up a note in a reasonable facsimile of Dan's squarish handwriting: "For my lovely bride!"

Elsie rubbed her palms together. "I need to get there on

the early side to help set up, so I'll just nip over to the hall with this and the bowl of salad I signed up to bring."

Noah said, "Let me know how this goes."

"You're not coming?" Elsie's eyes widened. "No, this is unacceptable. I will make sure you're there." She pulled out her phone. "Skye will say you should come. It's a potluck, for heaven's sake."

It took two minutes. By the time Noah returned from putting the cake in Elsie's car, she was holding up her phone. "You're coming!"

He folded his arms and leaned in the doorway. "Just what I needed—another event."

She slipped up closer and pressed against him so he automatically took her in his arms. "But you'll do it for me?"

Right now, he'd have done anything for her. He brushed his lips over her forehead. "You've convinced me."

She got on her toes and kissed him quick. "Show up at six. I'll keep Skye occupied until dessert. Besides, you don't want to miss out on everyone's reaction to the cake."

True. But more than that, Noah didn't want to miss out on Elsie. Not when he finally had a chance.

CHAPTER ELEVEN

Skye huffed. "Elsie, I'm right here. Quit checking your phone!"

Elsie shoved her phone in her pocket and pushed a cart of floral arrangements into the hall to set on the tables. Any time someone arrived with new food, Elsie intercepted it and carried it into the kitchen area. As far as Skye and her mother were concerned, food just kept appearing.

Which had made it super easy to step outside, pop into the car, and carry in the sealed cat litter cake.

Mrs. Bluett took the flowers from Elsie and set them out on the tables, so Elsie headed back to the buffet and lit the Sterno cans. Everything looked awesome. Including Skye, who kept finding new things to panic about and then rushing back to fix them. The thing Skye wanted to fix most seemed to be Elsie. "Are you okay? Why are you checking the phone every two minutes? Is there an emergency?"

"No, sorry." Elsie didn't have a reason to keep checking the phone—except for Noah. And right now it felt wrong to blurt out to Skye, "By the way, I know this week should be all about you and Dan, but I seem to have restarted things with the guy I never entirely left behind."

As the Maid of Honor, Elsie needed to put the bride's feelings and needs first, all the time, constantly, until the last person left the reception hall and the bride was on the plane to her honeymoon. That meant not dismaying her by saying she'd gotten back together with her ex.

It was just—Noah was fun over text. He always had been, with those cute quips and his voice coming through even in short messages. And sometimes he'd serve her the setup of a one-liner, and she'd return the serve, and she'd smile. It felt comfortable.

He'd changed. He'd gone to college, gotten a job, and changed everything about himself. Eight years apart had done what eight years together wouldn't have.

The doors opened, and Dan arrived with Kevin and a bunch of groomsmen. "Nice to show up," Elsie muttered.

"They had an issue over at the tuxedo fitting." Skye huffed. "The store got the colors wrong, but Dan said it wasn't a problem. It's just that straightening it out meant they were late for everything else all day."

Elsie paused, because—well, part of the deal was not to hurt Skye. But did it hurt Skye when Dan's schedule got thrown to the wolves?

While the volume level rose in the main hall, Elsie went back into the kitchen to check off which food had arrived and which hadn't. Some of the groomsmen darted in with bags of chips and dips (*Thanks!*) and a few brought sodas. Elsie carried those to the drink table.

There in the corner, alongside a big batch of homemade cookies, stood the box with the cake, and Dan's note. *Can we just skip to dessert?*

Here, Elsie did check her phone. Noah had sent her a selfie as Edgar Chantz. "I look ready to go into the studio," he'd added.

Oh, wow, did he ever? He'd jacked up his hair so it fell forward, and he'd made up his eyes to get that dusky Edgar Chantz expression. He was even pouting at the camera as if attempting to set it on fire. Then there was the clothing, which they'd absolutely nailed back in high school: the tight black jeans, the black workboots, and the grey t-shirt with the sleeves rolled up. He was holding a guitar, to complete the effect.

Noah's ability to step into a role had been one of the most enchanting things about him, back in high school, how he knew the best ways to become the thing he needed to become. Although that was a bit worrisome, too, because in all that time, he never did seem to know what he himself was becoming. He became Edgar Chantz for the Halloween parade, sure. But he became the Lord of Mischief for Dan, and apparently now he had become a high-level hacker for his employer.

Elsie didn't want him to become anything for her. She wanted to know who he was—himself.

That was too much for a text. She sent only, "Are you going to play that thing for us?"

"Elsie! The phone!" Skye blew into the kitchen. "Do I need to encase it in concrete and sink it into the sea?"

"Pretty sure that voids the warranty." Elsie closed her message window so Skye's Edgar Chantz radar wouldn't immediately ping in the presence of her favorite musician. "You were joking around with the groomsmen. What harm could it do?"

"Please." Skye dragged Elsie by the arm. "Come say hi to my grandmother."

The phone vibrated in Elsie's pocket while she met up with the other bridesmaids who'd just arrived, and then she chatted with Skye's grandmother, and then she had to take pictures. Relatives kept arriving, but they grabbed snacks from the snack table and poured their own drinks. Elsie joined with Skye's mom to carry food out to the catering trays.

Noah showed up, looking un-Chantzy. "The place looks

nice. You did a great job."

"Thanks." Elsie looked him up and down. "No guitar?"

"You're so mean. I texted you that I was, in fact, practicing one of the only guitar riffs I ever managed to learn." He mock pouted. "Except you were busy setting up this place for a hundred guests, so I had to cope with being ignored."

"You're adorable when you're pretending to be the center of the universe."

Noah's eyebrows raised. "Are you saying I'm not?"

Dan strode up behind Noah and dropped an arm on his shoulder. "You can't be the center of the universe."

"I forgot—because *you're* at the center, and unless we're both in the same place—"

Dan cut him off. "Nice gag with the tuxedos. We fixed it up."

"Bummer. Everyone would have remembered orange."

Dan met Elsie's eyes. "I blame you. You insisted we invite this joker."

Elsie opened her hands and shrugged. "Your friendship deserves a second chance."

Dan said, "I'll take that under advisement, but to the best of my knowledge, it didn't really end. Noah just never came home."

Noah's eyes glinted.

Dan turned to him. "However—I've had enough of you. You wanted my attention, and you've gotten it. Tomorrow, I want you with me the whole day. Show up at the house at nine o'clock because we're going on a whale watch."

Noah frowned. "We're doing what?"

"They say to keep your friends close and your enemies closer. Right now I'm not sure which you are, but either way, you're coming with me. Otherwise I have no idea what trouble you're getting into."

Noah made an innocent face.

Dan raised his eyebrows. "I'm all for good pranks, but I'm also for outwitting my opponent when possible. If you want to turn it into a battle of wits, that's fine, but you'll do it from a boat."

Noah gestured in the direction of the ocean. "And then you push me overboard?"

Dan rubbed his chin. "See, that was Kevin's style, not yours. You upgraded me from the practical joke straight into the meta-cognitive zone. Your pranks were about doing the unexpected so the other person questioned reality. Shoving someone into the ocean might feel good, but you'd much rather reprogram my car radio so it plays only Supertramp."

Noah's eyebrows raised.

"Right. So tomorrow, you're with me. Nine o'clock, at the house. You'll get in the car with me. You'll get on the boat with me. And afterward, you'll go to the rehearsal with me."

Noah made a devastated face. "Sounds like you're threatening me with a good time."

Dan grinned. "I hope so."

After he walked away, Noah said to Elsie, "So, what unexpected thing shall we do on the whale watch."

"Not me. The bridesmaids are having a spa day. The whole thing—hair, nails, massages. Skye wants everything totally relaxed."

Elsie snuck a look across the hall to where Skye was standing with her hands wrapped around one another and her eyes huge—the very picture of what you'd envision on hearing the words, "Totally relaxed."

Noah observed, "She may need five massages after we unveil dessert."

Once the food was open, Noah was…everywhere. Wherever Elsie turned, Noah seemed to be chatting up a random guest or one of the bridesmaids, always with his phone in his hand. "Potlucks can be such a weird mix," he was always saying to whichever person he'd collared. "But it looks like they've got everything covered. See, Skye's aunt provided that tray of wings," and he'd be pointing to the phone screen, showing the person the signup website, "and Dan's mom is who to thank for the awesome little mozzarella balls with tomato and basil."

Then Noah "accidentally" air-dropped a screenshot of the menu to every phone in the building. Because of course he did. No one was reading it too closely. They noted what it was while Noah apologized from the bottom of his heart. How clumsy.

Dan was giving Noah wicked side-eye, and Elsie kept repressing her smile. Meanwhile, Skye was in her glory, animatedly introducing Elsie to all the distant relatives who'd flown or driven in, and so happy. The first time around, Skye had gotten her heart destroyed, and now, she was all delight.

Noah disappeared. How long would it take him to transform into Edgar Chantz?

Not too long, apparently. Elsie's phone buzzed. "Get Skye out in the middle of the room."

Skye was talking to two grey-haired men Elsie didn't recognize, so she inserted herself into the conversation and got introduced to Skye's uncles. *Hi, nice to meet you, heard so much about you, how's it going?* "The food is awesome, isn't it?" Elsie said.

One of the uncles pulled out his phone. "So glad for the menu right here, otherwise I'd never have known what tabouleh was."

Elsie snickered. "Or whom to thank for introducing you to it?"

"Oh, I'd have guessed it was Skye's older sister. She's always been so darned healthy." Both men laughed.

Elsie said, "Speaking of healthy, we should check on dessert."

"Do you think so?" But Skye let Elsie lead her away anyhow. "Everyone's still eating. There was a line at the buffet a few minutes ago."

When they got out to the middle of the room, the lights dimmed, and a guitar chord sounded.

Elsie couldn't smother her grin as Skye pivoted straight toward the door. That was one of those, "I can name that song in one note" chords—the opening chord of Edgar

Chantz's most popular song.

Not Skye's favorite song, but still—the most distinctive. And quite possibly the only one Noah knew how to play.

In strode Edgar Chantz, each footfall bold. "Skye?" he called, his voice a question but with that thick Maine accent that set him apart in the rock world. "Skye Sanderson?"

Skye's sister exclaimed, "Whoa! Is that Edgar Chantz?"

As if Edgar Chantz walked around everywhere he went holding a guitar. Maybe everyone thought he went to the grocery store with a guitar, in case the checkout was long and he got inspired. But Noah had a point—give people visually what they expect, and they won't think about it. Not much.

Edgar stopped right before Skye. "I can't let you get away from me."

Skye's hand gripped Elsie's so tightly.

Edgar pulled a bunch of folded papers from his back pocket. "All of these—you wrote me over and over, but I never answered. I let you get away, Skye."

Skye had sent letters—bunches. When she was really young. No one was going to add up the years.

"I made a mistake." Edgar's voice broke. "You poured out your heart, and I didn't listen. I didn't value what you were giving to me."

Dan strode across the room. "Skye!"

Skye turned to Dan, arms folded. "Hush! I'm being courted by my first-ever crush."

She was grinning, and Noah nearly broke into a laugh, too. Nearly. Dan gave an Oscar-worthy eye-roll, which nearly set Elsie into laughter.

Skye raised her voice. "Edgar, you're too late. I've found the man of my dreams."

Edgar projected his voice, which Noah had been trained to do during drama club. "Give me a chance, darling!"

Skye gestured to the letters, carefully folded so no one could see they'd all been written in the last three hours. "You already had your chance."

Edgar looked right into Elsie's eyes, and all of a sudden, she saw Noah. It wasn't that the makeup or the costume were flawed—they weren't. But in that moment, Elsie stood heart-to-heart with Noah, despite the years and despite the way he'd hidden from her and despite everything, here they both were.

"I'm asking for *another* chance," he said, voice growly like Edgar but still Noah, just Noah right there in front of her. "An opportunity to be worthy of the woman who's proven she's worth everything—a woman who should have stood at the center of my world if only I'd been the man she needed me to be."

Dan snorted. Skye gave him a shove. "Quit that. I'm being praised, and you should be proud I've already chosen you."

Noah—Edgar—went on, "All this time, I should have been with you, and instead I was wrapped up in myself. But if I can have another chance—a real chance—then I promise, I'll make it up to you."

Chills crawled up Elsie's spine. Elsie said, "How can you make up for all those lost years?"

Edgar turned to her. "One shot. An honest listen, and a willing heart."

Dan muttered, "I like it better when someone else is writing your lyrics."

"I like it just fine." Skye giggled. "Edgar, you're amazing, but I'm afraid it's not in the cards for us. I've got my happily ever after."

Edgar said, "Can you at least make your first dance one of my songs?"

Dan's fists clenched. Skye side-eyed him. "I tried, but *someone* wanted a different song."

Dan said, "That's not fair."

Edgar said, "Well, no accounting for taste. If you marry me, you could have any first dance you like."

Skye pulled out her phone and took a selfie with Edgar. Several people, in fact, were taking photos of her with Edgar. Edgar pulled off his characteristic pout, and it was a masterpiece. "No photos with anyone else," Edgar growled. "Only with my beloved. And maybe with her beloved, too."

Dan opted out. It was just as well—his frown would have ruined the photos.

Selfies taken, Skye raised her eyebrows. "You know, Edgar, if you want to sing for me, I'm all ears."

Elsie bit her lip because apparently Skye, too, had no problem pranking a prankster. For the first time, Dan smirked.

Edgar shifted the guitar around front and strummed a chord. Noah was nowhere near as good as the real Edgar Chantz, but he knew how to strum a G.

Now, whether Noah could sing? That was another question entirely.

In a low voice, Dan said, "Why don't you escape right now with your dignity intact?"

Noah replied, in a voice equally low, "Why don't you let your fiancée enjoy her fantasy?"

Dan folded his arms, but Skye clasped her hands and bounced on her toes. "Please?"

Noah strummed a bit, and then he started one of Chantz's few ballads. He must have practiced this (poor Mrs. Edgemont, hearing it all through her vents) but singing and playing at the same time—that was hard. Unless he'd kept up with guitar playing through the years. It had never occurred to Elsie to ask.

And the song he'd chosen—well, there were no "simple" Edgar Chantz songs, but this one was slower, and the opening didn't have a dozen time signature changes. Plus, it was all about a broken heart. *You deserved the stars, and I gave you the dark,* went the song. *You wanted the moon, and I locked up my heart.*

Edgar watched his hands, but every so often, he did look up—and when he did, it wasn't at Skye. It was at Elsie.

He'd abandoned her to the dark. He wanted to do better.

To most effectively annoy Dan, Noah should have played Skye's suggested first dance song. Instead, Noah was asking Elsie for her heart. For forgiveness. For an erasure of the last eight years.

Edgar ran to the end of the first chorus, then said, "You sure, darling?"

"It's still a no." She hugged Edgar around the guitar, then whispered in his ear. Edgar—Noah—grinned, then turned to Dan with a smile. "You've got a fine woman here. Enjoy your dessert."

Dan glowered. "Screw off."

Elsie giggled. Edgar walked out, turning the lights back on as he left.

Skye's mother slid over. "Was that really—?"

Skye laughed. "It was our favorite celebrity impersonator."

Elsie said, "What did you say to him at the end?"

"I told him, *I thought you were taller.*" Skye gave Dan a hug. "You're being so sour. You said you love a good prank, and that was hilarious."

Dan huffed off to sulk with Kevin, who laughed at him and then pounded the table. "Dude, just slink into the bushes in shame."

Turning to Elsie, Skye giggled. "You said something about opening up the dessert table, but it feels unfair to do that without *Edgar* in the room."

"You should have offered him a cookie."

Skye gasped. "No! Edgar never touches food within an hour of touching his guitar! He doesn't want to get grease on the wood."

Elsie raised her hands. "Right! Sorry. Well, let's give *Edgar* time to, um, get away."

Skye said, "Besides, Noah's going to be upset that he missed a rock star proposing to me while he was in the restroom, so at the very least, he should have his choice of cake pops."

It took about ten minutes before Noah returned. While Dan glared from his table, Elsie gave Noah a once-over and then cleared a little makeup he'd missed near the corner of his eye. "You'll never believe what happened."

Seeing Noah back, Skye yanked Dan by the arm to go

open the desserts, but Dan kept staring at Noah over his shoulder. Elsie hurried over to the dessert table, too. Because as much as she hated attention, attention was exactly necessary right now before the bride and groom could cover it back up.

Dan saw the box with his little note on it. "What the heck?" He tried to stop Skye from opening it. "I didn't bring anything."

Skye said, "You sound afraid Edgar Chantz is going to jump out of the cake," and she slid up the box top. And backed up with a gasp.

Elsie let out a scream.

Attention: gathered. But not on her—on the thing she was pointing to.

Skye's mother exclaimed, "What on earth is that?" and then Skye's sister said, "Oh!" and Elsie, wanting to make sure that cake got eaten, yanked the box top out of Skye's hands to reveal the cat litter box in all its gross glory.

Elsie exclaimed, "Oh, it's a cake!" and then dumped a vile-looking scoop onto a paper plate—and handed it to Skye.

Skye's mother said to Dan, "Why would you do that?"

With that, Elsie's work was done.

Noah's work was not. Over the next half-hour, Noah made sure to tell everyone, truthfully, "Dan denies all knowledge of a cat litter cake."

As the welcome party wound down, Elsie slipped up alongside Noah. "And yet, telling everyone Dan denied knowing about the cake somehow cemented him in everyone's mind as the provider of said cake."

Dan approached them, eyes dark.

Noah mocked concern. "Oh, dear. Not my intention at all."

Elsie whispered, just before Dan arrived, "That's the problem with being a jerk. Denying your jerkiness only convinces everyone even more that you did it."

Unamused, Dan pointed at Noah. "Tomorrow, you are not leaving my side."

Noah inclined his head. "Right by your side, the whole day."

The way Noah said it, Dan should have been afraid. And Elsie giggled.

CHAPTER TWELVE

"I've never been on a whale watch," was Noah's only comment as he slid into Dan's car.

"I hope you brought sunscreen and your best behavior." Dan didn't look to have forgiven Noah for the cake—although in Noah's opinion, both pranks had worked out about as well as they could have. By the end of the evening, not even one crumb remained of the cat litter cake. Sure, Skye's older relatives had wrinkled their noses and gone in search of the cake pops, but Dan's relatives? They'd given Dan all 100% of the credit for that cake, and in the true spirit of embracing a prank, they'd scooped up all the cat doots first. Kevin had eaten five servings, really hamming it up every time he found another chocolate "treat" in the cake. Dan's own grandfather had clapped him on the shoulder, proclaiming, "I'm glad to see you haven't lost your edge."

Moreover, from the start of the Edgar Chantz stuff, it

was obvious Skye knew what was up. If anything, she probably thought Dan had set that up, as well. Because he loved her.

Noah stared out the back window while Dan, Kevin, and one other groomsman played music and talked about people he didn't know. Last night aside, Elsie was right about Dan enjoying most of their pranks just as much as Noah enjoyed them. This was the problem—anything cruel enough that Dan wouldn't enjoy it wasn't something Noah wanted to do. So far, Noah and Elsie had inconvenienced Dan, but they hadn't made him question reality or feel all alone in the world. Not once had Dan come close to feeling the way Elsie had felt when she'd walked into a massive party held in her honor, in a way that made her feel so profoundly unheard.

Except they were running out of time. Tomorrow was the wedding. Today was the bridal party spa day (untouched by any pranks whatsoever) and the whale watch for the groomsmen. Tonight was the rehearsal and the rehearsal dinner, and Noah was out of ideas. Sure, he could call the cops on the rehearsal dinner if he wanted—and he kind of did—but that wasn't going to cause any massive hardship. And as Dan said, Noah had never been a "practical joke" kind of guy. Kevin would think setting off the fire alarm in the wedding venue would be a hilarious gag. True pranks had to involve the brain. They had to be unexpected. They had to be both surprising and funny, and (hardest of all) they had to be funny long outside the moment.

In freshman year of high school, Dan would have thought shoving someone into a swimming pool was an amazing prank. (Hint: that kind of thing was never funny.) By senior year, Dan and Noah had come up with the most amazing senior prank of all time—and no one got dunked.

Lasting harm wasn't a prank. It was harm.

The whole drive, Noah kept flipping that around in his head. Keeping Dan off-balance wasn't what Elsie wanted to achieve—but achieving what she outright said she wanted wasn't the kind of thing Noah liked to do. Elsie's prank ideas had always been perfect: fill the VP's office with canned goods, then donate the food. Make it funny, but in the end, no harm done—or, in fact, harm averted. Inconvenience people, sure, but leave them laughing. Tell them, "It's muggy outside," and then have them open the front door to find all their mugs lined up on the steps.

The third groomsman, a forgettable guy named John, turned toward Noah. "So, what's this senior prank Dan told me about?"

Dan said, "How could you not have heard? It was epic."

"I was in Michigan, and somehow people weren't talking about a tiny-town high school prank from a thousand miles away."

Noah huffed. "Then we failed."

Kevin said, "We did not fail. But it was wild."

Dan said, "Okay, so this tiny-town high school never had money for anything. The school couldn't raise money to save our lives, and the district wouldn't upgrade something unless the previous item was in pieces and no longer functional."

Noah said, "Every one of the water fountains had no pressure, so the water just kind of bubbled up a quarter inch from the spigot. That kind of thing."

Kevin said, "The drama club couldn't use the stage curtain because one side didn't close."

When John nodded, Dan said, "We liked the lunch ladies. They were fun, and they liked us, too, but their equipment was garbage. They were supposed to wheel out fruit on these carts every day, but the cart wheels didn't work, and they all lurched to one side or another. At least one of them collapsed mid-service."

Noah said, "The lunch ladies weren't strangers to our stunts, by the way. Like, you could buy soup crackers for five cents if you bought soup. But one day, Kevin walked in with ten dollars and came out of there with his tray piled with two hundred packets of soup crackers."

John laughed. Kevin said, "What can I say? I like soup

crackers."

Dan sped up as he talked. "Around January, one of the lunch carts tipped over and ended up spilling stuff everywhere, and while Noah helped the lunch lady clean it up, he got an idea."

Noah said, "The seniors always did a senior gift, so why not combine the senior gift and the senior prank?"

"We raised funds for four months," Dan said. "Car washes, selling cookies. We did singing telegrams and poked a thousand forks into people's lawns in order to raise donations—the whole nine yards."

Kevin said, "We did everything short of selling our souls, and we raised four grand."

Noah said, "The day before graduation, the high school seniors hold what they call a rolling rally. The other three years of students stand outside, and the teachers and admins, and all the seniors decorate their cars and drive around the school, honking like mad, and then we'd drive up Main Street and be a general nuisance."

Dan said, "We broke into the school the night before and took every single lunch cart. The small ones with the busted wheels, the large one that would have rolled into the walk-in if it moved at all, the horrible racks that should be holding glasses—every one of them."

John exclaimed, "Seriously?"

Kevin said, "We could have gotten in so much trouble, but it was worth it."

Noah said, "There were like thirty cars in the rolling rally, and the first seven were each towing one of those awful carts."

John hit the dashboard. "Awesome!"

Dan said, "The principal was livid. I thought she was going to step into the lineup and stop us all right there, but it was seven o'clock in the morning, and she knew full well we'd all be back in the school in half an hour. So there we were, circling the building with these carts, blowing air horns. The big carts were fastened into a couple of pickup trucks. Two of the carts broke free of their tethers, so after that we had a few guys running and pushing them around the lot."

Noah said, "The ones that didn't let go? The wheels went, and we were just dragging scrap metal by the end."

"So, afterward, the whole senior class is standing in front of the doors while the principal yells at us that we're in trouble for vandalizing school property and maybe she's going to cancel graduation and we should be ashamed of ourselves. And she marches us into the lunch room to apologize to the lunch ladies—and there were all the new carts."

Noah said, "We'd preemptively replaced every one of the ones we destroyed, plus bought a couple others the head of food service said would be really useful."

Kevin said, "I had an aunt who worked for a restaurant supply company, so she hooked us up with whatever we needed."

Dan snickered. "We'd told them our senior gift was going to be a memorial rocking chair for the library. They thought our senior prank was massive destruction of school property." He glanced in the rear view mirror and met Noah's eyes. "Instead it was kitting out the lunch ladies because they'd been nice to us all those years—and all of our friends working together to accomplish it."

———

There was time for one more really good prank—if Noah could come up with it. Twenty-four hours until the wedding, which he couldn't touch. That left the rehearsal dinner, if only he could plan the right prank.

Since last night, though, he hadn't been able to come up with anything to make Dan feel like all his allies had abandoned him.

Or, for that matter, even make Dan feel the way Noah had felt: deceived, and made the inadvertent instrument of someone else's pain.

Instead, Dan was in the car, laughing about old pranks

and how those pranks had cemented their friendships. Not the impression he wanted to leave.

Noah texted Elsie. "We need something big for the rehearsal dinner."

Elsie replied, "Such as?"

"I'm at a loss. Whatever it is, you're going to need to do all the legwork."

"Except I'm at the spa day."

Noah sighed. "We could order twenty-five pizzas to the rehearsal dinner."

"I can't imagine the restaurant would let them in the door."

True. "We could issue an open invitation for everyone in Brighthead to get autographs from the entire Marvel Cinematic Universe, conveniently at the same time as the rehearsal."

Elsie sent a laughing smilie.

"Do you have ten friends with black suits, sunglasses, and earpieces? They could escort Dan out of the rehearsal."

Elsie replied, "Blast. I wish we'd thought of this sooner. My cousins would have done it."

At the pier, Dan led his troop over to a fifty-six foot catamaran. They started loading it up with food and music and anything else that qualified as entertainment. As more of Dan's relatives arrived, Noah pieced together that this was a private charter—hence why it was no big deal for Dan to add Noah at the last minute—and they'd leave when everybody had arrived. The whale watch would be three hours.

But it didn't have to be.

The crew consisted of the captain (the pilot?) as well as a tour guide and someone who'd be working concessions. Noah approached them with a huge smile. "Is it still possible to opt for the longer tour?"

That was a guess on his part, but it paid off.

The captain said, "Yes, but I thought you had a hard return time so you could get to the wedding rehearsal."

Noah beamed. "We changed the schedule, so we're actually free for up to six hours."

"We only go to five, but if you want five, we head go out pretty far, maybe see some whales we don't normally get a chance to view when we stay closer to home."

Noah pulled out his wallet. "You know, that sounds like just the thing."

He paid cash. A lot of cash, but who cared? The captain said to the tour guide, "You're good for five hours?"

The tour guide laughed. "Talking about whales for five hours? Not even a challenge."

Noah laid on the charm. "You have no idea how much we appreciate this."

"We" being him and Elsie, of course. Maybe Dan would appreciate it eventually. Maybe Noah had finally found the thing that would leave Dan feeling off-balance and betrayed.

CHAPTER THIRTEEN

Dan started the trip by sequestering Noah's phone. "Because I know you, and you're going to post some garbage to my social media just before we get far enough from shore that we no longer have cell phone service."

Noah laid a hand on his heart and made a sad face.

Last night, he'd posted to Dan's socials, "I think I have beautiful feet." This had immediately prompted a long discussion of Dan's toes, gratifying Noah when he'd checked at two o'clock in the morning. Always good when the chief jackal was surrounded by jackals just as ready-to-pounce as himself. The status was gone by four a.m.

Noah handed over his phone. "And you? You're not setting aside your phone, too? How is that fair?"

Dan rolled his eyes. "I'm not interested in fairness. I'm interested in locking you down so you can't cause any damage."

Noah followed him to the upper deck. "I haven't done

any damage."

Dan turned to him. "That's why I find you so frustrating. Because you're threatening damage, and you keep pulling your punches. I know you could have wiped all my devices or deleted my accounts or hacked my credit cards to purchase Portugal—but instead you're baking cakes and hiring a balloon animal artist."

Noah recoiled. "What makes you think I baked that cake?"

"Intelligence, that's what makes me think it." Dan tilted his head. "Shut up and watch the whales. And don't push anyone overboard."

Noah laid a hand on his heart. "I promise, everyone's staying on the boat."

Dan grimaced. "I'm keeping you here because I don't want you messing with Skye while I'm on land and can't get to her. The Edgar Chantz stuff came too close to that. What if she'd believed you?"

Noah brightened. "You thought my impression was that good?"

"Dude, you suck as a guitar player, but that's the point—what if she'd believed it was him?"

"She chose you over him, hands-down. I'd call that an unqualified win in your column."

Dan powered down Noah's phone and put it in his pocket.

Noah prompted, "And your phone?"

Dan sighed.

"You've got a camera for photos," Noah pressed. "And you already said we'll be out of cell phone range."

"Fine." Dan took a selfie with the two of them, then posted it to social media. "If I drown," he typed, "I want the cops to find this man and prosecute."

Noah shook his head. "I'd never."

Dan said, "Now, I know you won't."

Not having their phones meant no one was really keeping an eye on the time. They were keeping an eye on the whales. They were keeping an eye on the food, and they were listening to the tour guide, and they were listening to the music. The catamaran had two decks. The upper deck was lined with benches so the whale-watchers could sit under a canopy in the breeze, reapplying sunscreen every so often and watching for whales. The lower deck became party central, with a TV screen, music, food, and a couple of tables.

Noah hung around the tour guide, who told them all about the whales they were seeing. "You can expect to see fin whales, minke whales, and humpback whales. If we're really lucky, you might even see a North Atlantic right whale."

She pulled out all sorts of exhibits, remarking that she didn't normally get a chance to go this in-depth. But here was some baleen, and these were fifteen uses of baleen, and here were items made of baleen. Here was a model of the sand lance, the fish most commonly eaten (by the ton!) by the whales in the Stellwagen Bank National Marine Sanctuary.

Meanwhile the captain would radio the upper deck every so often saying some other boat had spotted such-and-such in a certain area, so we'll be heading there now. Only at some point, their boat had outstripped all the other whale watches and were way out at sea.

Dan's guests got a quick tour of the engine room, which Noah imagined wasn't standard on the shorter tours—and that was interesting because the boat had a gyroscope and a computer calculating the water turbulence to stabilize the catamaran. A dozen questions later, Noah had to content himself with, "I don't know—it just does," and he cursed the fact that Dan had his phone—although he couldn't have looked it up anyhow.

Why? Because no one had cell service. Which meant no one realized how far out they were, nor how long it was going to take to head back to shore.

"Oh!" the tour guide exclaimed. "Look, fin whales! And they're spyhopping!"

Dan was up on the deck. "Spyhopping being...?"

The tour guide said, "See how they're just poking up their heads, vertical in the water? They're looking at us. We're a curiosity to them because we don't normally get out this far."

Dan snickered. "We got the special tour?"

Noah braced himself for the discovery phase.

The tour guide said, "You absolutely did. It's too bad the bride couldn't be here to see them, too. You'd have a cetacean send-off!"

"I asked. She wanted that spa day." Dan side-eyed Noah. "Unless you cancelled it."

Noah raised his hands. "Skye's the limit." He glanced at the whales watching the whale watch. "Skye-hopping's the limit?"

"Leave the puns to Elsie. She does them better."

Noah smirked, but Dan just walked away.

So—not the discovery phase. Not yet.

It took another half hour before Noah noticed people checking their phones, and people asking one another when they'd start seeing the shoreline so they could go home. The tour guide was still excitedly pointing out all the sea life, though—and yes, they'd seen minke whales. And sharks. All of it was amazing.

Finally Dan stalked over to Noah, eyes blazing, and Noah flattened his facial expression because the discovery phase had, indeed, arrived..

The catamaran had slowed and was beginning to make a turn.

"Come with me." Dan's voice was low, and Noah was instantly on high alert. Without any attempt at laughter or denial, Noah followed to the lower deck, and from there, Dan led him into the engine room and shut the door.

Well, if Dan killed him in here, at least it would be an interesting locked-room mystery for the detectives.

Dan faced him. "I said not to hurt Skye."

Noah opened his hands. "I assume right about now, Skye is getting a pedicure."

"Skye is going to lose her mind." Dan's voice was steely. "We have no cell phone service, and there is no way we can get back within range before the start of the wedding rehearsal."

Noah said, "So you'll wing it tomorrow?"

Dan stepped closer, his voice merging with the drone of the engine, which was beginning to speed up. "She's going to think I ditched her. She's been afraid of nothing more than being left at the altar for the past six months, and all along, I've promised her I'm not doing what the last guy did, and leaving her flat."

Noah recoiled. "What?"

"Don't play innocent. Elsie told you Skye got left at the altar two years ago—the guy's entire family just didn't show up."

Noah shook his head.

Dan closed the space between them. "This was too far—this was you hurting her. I wouldn't have cared if you swapped out my sunscreen with hand sanitizer or you replaced my tuxedo shirt with a toddler-sized shirt and pretended it shrank in the wash. Those things would have been funny—but this? This is not funny." He was breathing hard. "You realized her worst fear, and she's going to be sobbing—and instead of being there with her, I'm stuck with you!"

Noah raised his hands. "I had no idea about any of that!"

"I don't want to hear you lying about what you knew!" Dan's fists clenched. "You marched back into Brighthead with a smirk and a vendetta, and I have no idea what your problem is! You're acting like you want revenge on me, but then you're not actually getting revenge--but I wish you would just do it and get it over with so we can quit this game where you act like you're my friend, and in every other respect you're my enemy."

Noah's eyes narrowed. "You proved you weren't my friend back in high school."

"We left high school." Dan stepped toward the door. "If you've got any computer prowess that will enable me to get a message to the mainland, maybe you can do it now for me. Reprogram a satellite or something. I'm through with you."

He stalked out of the room, slamming the door and leaving Noah alone with the stabilizing gyroscope.

CHAPTER FOURTEEN

Elsie was sitting in her bedroom, arms around Skye while Skye sobbed, when both their phones buzzed simultaneously with an incoming text.

Skye fumbled her phone up, and then she was gasping, and crying a bit more. It was Dan. "We're coming back from the whale watch. Noah screwed up the boat, but we're coming."

Elsie stared at her screen. Skye was sobbing into her hands, so Elsie texted, "Got it. I'm here with her. What happened?"

Noah screwing up the boat—did he stall the engines? Hack the captain's GPS so they boated out to Nova Scotia?

Dan replied, "Your ex-boyfriend told the captain we'd opted for the five-hour tour, not the three-hour. Paid him cash. We were heading to London and only just got cell phone service back."

Hands shaking, Elsie texted, "I'm sorry."

Every text was showing up on Skye's phone, too. And now Elsie realized Dan had also group-texted Skye's parents.

A long gap. Skye texted into her phone, "You're coming back?"

It took a while for the reply, so Elsie said, "I bet reception is still garbage out there. Do you have location services for each other?"

Skye shook her head. "He offered. I told him not to."

It wouldn't have helped. The location tracker would have just told her Dan's last known location. She still could have thought he'd powered down his phone and abandoned her. Or the boat had sunk, and he'd died.

Noah.

Noah hadn't texted yet.

Noah had messed with Skye. He'd done something so ridiculous and awful that he'd left Skye in tears, and that—

Elsie had been texting Noah all day. The last few hours of texts had gone unread, and now she knew why. But even so—even so. She switched back to Noah's chat screen, and her messages had all switched to "delivered" but not "read."

The North Atlantic might be frigid, but so help her, Noah was in hot water.

Dan replied, "I'm definitely coming. I'll drive a hundred miles an hour, but I'm coming home to you."

Elsie texted, "How about you text us when you get in the car, and drive safely instead?"

It would be too late for the wedding rehearsal anyhow. Dan would have to join them at the rehearsal dinner. She said to Skye, "Let's go back outside. Let's at least go over everything we need to review even though Dan isn't here for it."

Tear-streaked, Skye looked up. "That was a terrible prank."

Elsie said, "I had no idea he was planning that."

"Dan kept Noah with him to prevent him from ruining the rehearsal." Skye swallowed. "But he did it anyhow."

Fists clenched in her lap, Elsie stared out the window. Noah had said he wouldn't harm Skye. Through the entire process, he'd kept saying, over and over, he'd respect Elsie's wish about not getting Skye caught up in the pranks. But here Skye had spent the last half hour sobbing, believing Dan had abandoned her the same way Alan had, and it was entirely the fault of Noah.

Noah, who hadn't kept his word. Who for the second time couldn't be trusted.

Both their phones buzzed again. "I'll drive safely. I promise."

A knock on the door, and Skye's mother stepped inside. Elsie patted Skye on the leg. "Let's get you cleaned up, and we can at least talk to the officiant. She may be able to come back later tonight after the rehearsal dinner."

"Yeah." Skye hugged her mom, then went into Elsie's en suite bathroom.

Skye's mom said, "I don't understand what happened. Who's your ex boyfriend, and why would he do that?"

Elsie's mouth tightened. "Noah. The Edgar Chantz impersonator last night."

"Oh! The young man who was Dan's partner in crime back in high school?" There was no way Skye's mom remembered that—Skye must have filled her in after last night's party. "But he was so nice to pretend to be Edgar Chantz. Why would he mess with the boat as a prank?"

Elsie muttered, "I have no idea what he was thinking."

Probably thinking he knew better than Elsie—again. Last time Noah got in trouble because he didn't believe in holding fast to what he wanted. This time, he got in trouble for holding fast to nothing while doing whatever he wanted. But really, the effect was the same: someone spent an hour crying.

And the other effect, also the same: Elsie hardened her heart.

Szymczak could just sail right back out to sea on that boat. Or, since Szymczak hadn't bothered texting Elsie yet, maybe Dan was handcuffing him to the cargo hold. Maybe

Dan would put Szymczak off in a lifeboat so a friendly dolphin could tug Szymczak over to Cape Cod.

It was odd that he hadn't texted, come to think of it. But whatever.

No, wait, not whatever. Elsie had been texting Szymczak all afternoon. So while Skye washed her face in the bathroom, Elsie stayed on her bed with her phone.

She'd spent the day planning. Elsie's cousins, always up for a laugh, did indeed own black suits and mirrored sunglasses. They'd cobbled together earpieces, and they'd agreed to arrest Dan at the rehearsal dinner. When they'd sent Elsie photos of their G-men getup, she'd forwarded those to Noah.

Szymczak needed one more message. Elsie texted, "It's off. That was a prank too far."

She added, "I'm cancelling the G-men, and don't you dare show up tonight."

Elsie texted her cousins next, and they both responded with disappointment. "I was looking forward to seizing several slices of pizza as evidence," replied one of them. "Are you sure we can't do it anyhow?"

It would be hilarious, except the one thing Elsie remembered about pranking was the mutuality: when one person said, "That's enough," then that was enough. Dan wasn't going to be up for another prank tonight. Skye certainly wasn't. And after tonight, Elsie was out of time.

Skye rejoined Elsie, looking wan but in control. "Let's go tell everyone the wedding's still on."

Elsie muttered, "And maybe a funeral."

Skye shook her head. "Dan won't hurt him."

Which was more than Elsie could say for herself right now. She texted Noah one more time, with, "Also, we're done."

That was hurting Noah in the worst way Elsie could think of. It just stank that it was going to hurt her, too.

Elsie found the rehearsal dinner, frankly, boring. But maybe after today's prank, boring was good. Everyone from Dan's side was exhausted from their extended whale-watch (sun and wind and sea took a lot out of you if you weren't used to it) and Skye's side was unnerved because of what had looked like a second runaway groom.

Skye flew toward Dan and hugged him, and he just shook his head, dark-eyed. Elsie approached.

"I didn't strand Szymczak at the dock." He frowned. "But I didn't want him in my car, so my uncle offered to drive him back to Brighthead."

"Whatever," Elsie said. "If he has to walk back to Massachusetts, it's all the same."

Once the restaurant opened up the buffet (no strawberries,) Skye and Dan got their food first, but Elsie hung back to chat with the other bridesmaids. Because Brighthead was such a small place, one of them was dating Kevin, the best man, and Kevin was regaling everyone with whale-tales as Elsie got closer. "You know how Dan goes off when he's mad?" Kevin laughed. "Not this time. He was dead silent. No one wanted to talk to him, and I don't blame them."

Kevin's girlfriend Jen said, "You said Dan liked pranks."

"Yeah, not this one, although I thought it was brilliant. Like anyone actually needs to rehearse a wedding." Kevin snorted. "You walk in, do your stuff at the front with the officiant, and walk out again. Oh, and you may kiss the bride."

Jen gave a roll of her eyes. "There was more to it than that."

"Unless we've got a dance routine and someone reciting a Shakespeare monologue, it's all the same." Kevin arched his eyebrows. "Everyone knows there are a thousand rules about weddings. Don't wear white. Give a gift that covers your plate. Don't upstage the bride."

Jen giggled, and Elsie glanced at her, wondering what was up with that.

Kevin straightened his shoulders. "The point is, if

everyone knows all those things, then of course we also know to march in, stand looking solemn, and march out again. Oh, and hand over the ring when it's time."

Elsie lowered her voice. "Don't you dare hide the ring from Dan."

"Noah ruined that gag for me. It would have been funny to go patting all my pockets looking for it, but after today, I think I'd get punched in the jaw." Kevin looked thoughtful. "I should be mad at Noah, but darn, when people finally realized it was past three hours and we were still motoring out in an easterly direction...? That was hilarious. I'd never have come up with that."

That was as good a time as any to get out of the conversation, so Elsie noticed aloud that the buffet line was shorter, and she took off. Five minutes later, with her plate loaded up, she scanned the tables for a decent seating option. Not with Kevin and Jen. Not with Skye's family. Deciding she wanted to be alone with her angry thoughts, Elsie picked a spot at a table some people had already abandoned, and one at a time she speared the tiny appetizers with her fork.

Her heart hurt. It really felt for a while like she and Noah could get back together. He certainly kissed like a man who wanted their relationship to go the distance.

Maybe she'd been fooling herself. Maybe he was thinking extremely short-term—as in, see if he could get her to stay the night before the wedding, and maybe the night after, and then ride off into the sunset, back to his commute and his computer.

The scrape of a chair startled Elsie, and she turned to find Dan settling himself in with a dessert plate laden with two pieces of pie. "You're all alone," he said, and that was just a statement so Elsie didn't bother replying. "What do you and Noah think you're doing?"

Elsie's shoulders tensed. "Did he say I made him do that?"

"I'm the one asking the questions." Dan kept eating, and gestured she should do the same. He swallowed another bite of pie, then continued, "You're the only reason he's in Brighthead. You made Skye invite him. He declined the invitation. Skye told you he wasn't coming, and the next morning, bam, we've got Szymczak incoming. This has your fingerprints all over it. So, what are you doing?"

Elsie took her time chewing a barbecue chicken leg that suddenly had no taste. "I will swear on a stack of Bibles that I had nothing to do with Noah sending you out to sea."

"I'm pretty sure you're the strawberry planner, and you're the one who sent me to three florists looking for a hydrangea brace. Both of which were pretty funny," he added. "I have to assume you gave Szymczak the keys to the router and that's how he's sniffing my passwords. Again, everything he's posted is pretty funny, although I suspect that's illegal and I could make him lose his job over it." Dan waved a hand. "But I'm chill. You, though— you're the one I don't get. I made Noah promise not to hurt Skye, and since you were working together, that promise should have included you."

Elsie said, "Even before you said anything, I made him promise not to hurt Skye, too."

"Except Skye did get hurt, so I need you to talk to me. What is going on?"

Elsie said, "You don't believe Noah?"

"Noah didn't tell me anything!" Dan's eyes blazed. "He wouldn't crack, so I walked away because my next response was going to be throwing him face-first into the wall."

Elsie recoiled. "You said he implicated me."

"No, I said your fingerprints were all over this. You went ahead and implicated yourself." Dan looked right at her over his pie plate. "I know you hate the spotlight, but I'm looking right at you. Talk."

While he ate, Elsie returned to a completely tasteless plate of food she didn't want to touch—except that eating meant she didn't have to respond right away. And there was no good response.

At least Szymczak had kept his promise not to implicate her.

Skye popped over, all smiles. "This is a nice party! It's so much more relaxed than yesterday's potluck because I'm not in charge of the food."

Elsie forced a smile. "You weren't in charge of the food yesterday, either."

"Well, no, Mom was in charge of the food, and you helped a lot."

Dan said, "And Elsie baked that cat litter cake."

Elsie sighed. "Dan."

Dan turned to Skye as she pulled her chair close to his. "Elsie and I are talking about how she and Szymczak have been in cahoots about these pranks the whole time, and she admitted this last one went too far."

Elsie wouldn't look at Skye. "Again, I had nothing to do with the whale watch. That came out of his demented head."

Skye's voice was quiet. "You were pranking our wedding?"

Dan said, "Elsie recruited Szymczak to come in and do it for her...except for the things she did on her own."

Skye said, "Why?"

Elsie's stomach tightened. "Noah wasn't supposed to involve you."

"I'm Dan's bride. Of course it was going to involve me." Skye's hand wove around Dan's, her fingers through his. "You're my Maid of Honor. You're letting me use your mom's house. Unless you don't want me to use your mom's house...?"

Dan said, "This is because of the birthday prank. Eight years later, you still haven't let it go."

Elsie's head whipped up. "And that's exactly why I haven't let it go—because eight years later, you still don't have a single regret about what you did. You humiliated me, and you got Noah in trouble, and you broke us up—and to you, it was just a hoot. What a funny prank as your capstone project before you swanned off to college to ruin people's lives there."

Skye gasped, "Elsie—?"

Elsie glared at Dan. "The aggressor does *not* get to tell the victim she's wrong for not getting over it, are we clear? Alan would have no right to tell Skye to get over her fear of abandonment, and you have no right to tell me to get over the fact that you upended my life."

Dan tilted his head. "Excuse me?"

Elsie sat forward, and she lowered her voice even as she sharpened it. "I'm not over it because everything you did had a lasting effect. Noah and I broke up over your prank. Maybe we'd have broken up eventually anyhow, but maybe we wouldn't have. We'll never know because you steamrolled him and then laughed your way out of town on the way to college orientation. You didn't pay the price for your prank—and you're the one who forgot Noah's primary rule, which was that at the end of a good prank, everyone walks away laughing."

Dan said, "You had a great time at that party!"

"You mean before you called the cops on us? I had the worst time holding it together and trying not to look like an ungrateful brat who didn't appreciate what her boyfriend had done for her. I didn't want the attention, and I didn't want the noise—and I certainly didn't want the cops."

Dan raised his hands. "I didn't call the cops."

Elsie rolled her eyes. "Oh, spare me. You didn't call the cops the same way I didn't mix pudding for a cat litter cake."

Dan shook his head. "That wasn't me."

"You blamed me for the whale watch prank on the grounds that I brought Noah back to Brighthead. I'm blaming you for the cops on the grounds that the party wouldn't have existed if you hadn't tricked Noah into throwing it."

She didn't break eye contact with Dan the whole time. Eight years of fury and helplessness were at a rolling boil. Elsie said, "I told Skye right at the start that you were bad news, and she told me you'd grown up and you'd changed. She's my friend, so I'll support her no matter what she does—even if she's making a mistake, I'm going to be right there with her. I asked her on day one what she'd do if you decided to skip out on her wedding as a prank, and she said you would never."

Skye said softly, "I listened to you. I told Dan I didn't care if he pranked me, but not to prank me that way."

Dan said, "Which I never did."

Elsie said, "Skye asked to use the beach house for the wedding—sure. She's my friend. She asked me to be Maid of Honor—sure. Anything for my friend. But you?" She raised her eyebrows. "Szymczak liked the idea of getting back at you. But we had rules. Nothing touching Skye. Nothing that would cost you money. Nothing on the actual day of the wedding."

Dan folded his arms and sat back, chin down.

Skye said, "Do you want not to be my Maid of Honor anymore? If you can't support the marriage, I mean?"

Elsie said, "I will support you to the ends of the earth. If you want me to step down, I'll do it right now. But him?" She turned to Dan. "You deserve whatever Noah dished out to you."

Skye squeezed Dan's hand as she said, "I don't want you to step down. But you never said any of this before."

Elsie said, "Then you weren't listening."

"You weren't this clear." Skye bit her lip. "You said you had reservations. You kept asking me if I was sure. You— I don't know, you didn't say all this."

Elsie folded her arms and sat back. "It wouldn't have changed your mind."

"Early on, it might have." Again Skye tightened her fingers around Dan's. "You don't believe me that he grew up, but even Dan will tell you that."

Dan had lowered his voice. "I didn't intend to break you two up. I did think it would be awesome to have one last, big party before all of us scattered to college, and have Noah foot the bill. And I did think you needed to loosen up. It was wrong to do all that at your expense."

Elsie waited him out.

"I'm sorry. What else do you want me to say?"

"I was waiting for the *I'm sorry*." Her eyes narrowed. "You asked what we were trying to do, and we were trying to even the score." She remembered what Noah had said, and added, "Not fully even because we didn't want to stop the wedding. But get a bit more even. I'm also pissed at Szymczak because we had an awesome prank planned for tonight, and I cancelled it."

Skye and Dan leaned forward while Elsie went through her phone to find the photos of her cousins in black with sunglasses and earpieces. "They were going to arrest you," she said, and Dan laughed so loud they got attention from the neighboring tables. "Then they'd have held you in my great uncle's ancient Towncar with the engine running and the windows up."

Skye was giggling. "Oh, that would have been hilarious."

"I don't know if they'd have left the parking lot, but my cousin suggested driving you for ice cream." Elsie bit her lip. "After Noah took you out to sea, you wouldn't have been in the mood for it, so, yeah, not happening now."

"Blast. Think of the stories!" Dan shook his head. "See, Noah screwed it all up."

"You're not getting it. *You* screwed everything up. I don't think Noah made it all that much worse."

Dan said, "Except neither of you ever said anything. You avoided me, and Noah never came back to Brighthead. When I met you again, you didn't put a little poison in my coffee every time we met. You just—simmered."

Skye said to Elsie, "And that's not fair. You didn't say how much it bothered you."

Dan said, "Which, by the way—did you actually tell Noah what Alan did to Skye?"

Elsie's eyes crinkled. "What do you mean? Of course I told him."

"He claimed he didn't know Skye got left at the altar. Did you 'tell him' tell him? Or did you kind of hint at it and expect he understood what you meant because of telepathy, the same way you assumed Skye knew you hated me because you told her you had reservations?"

Elsie sat back, frowning.

Had she explicitly said, "Don't mess with the ceremony because Skye got left at the altar"?

"I think I said Skye had been engaged and gotten her heart broken." Elsie bit her lip. "But I'm sure I told him."

"He's sure you didn't."

Skye said, "That would kind of change things."

Would it? Elsie pushed back her chair and took her plate. "No. This is too much."

She walked it to the trash can and dumped half a plate of food. She and Noah had talked so much about the rules around the actual pranks, but had she ever laid out exactly what happened to Skye? Why she hadn't objected so hard when Dan stepped in? Why she'd promised to give Skye whatever she wanted for her wedding, since the "wedding of her dreams" had ended in humiliation?

She came back to the table as Dan was getting up from his chair. "I'm sorry. I have no idea if I told Noah explicitly about Alan."

Dan folded his arms. "Have you heard from him since the whale watch?"

"I told him off, and then I blocked him."

Dan turned to Skye, who gave him a thumbs-up. He said to Elsie, "I'm sorry about the birthday prank. You're right that it was selfish. It's been eight years, and I figured you'd moved on because I'd moved on, but I should have apologized before now. It was a selfish stunt, and I'm sorry I hurt you."

Elsie said, "Apology accepted," and he inclined his head, then turned to go.

Skye said, "Do you want to step down as Maid of Honor?"

Elsie took her seat again. "No. Only if you want me gone."

"Well, I don't. Just—it sounds like you've never been

honest with me." With her hands folded, Skye looked so small. "I need to know I can trust you to speak up. To be fully honest, even if I don't know to ask you the right questions. Friendship is supposed to be about trust and comfort."

Elsie said, "I'm sorry."

Skye waved a hand. "You told me you broke up with Noah because you couldn't trust that he'd listen to you. You didn't feel safe around him. Well, I need to feel safe around you, too. I'll listen to you—but that means you have to speak."

Maybe Noah had reached the same conclusion—that if Elsie weren't speaking to him, he needed someone else to tell him the things she wasn't saying. It left the door wide open for Dan to tell Noah whatever he wanted, and then Noah believed it.

"You didn't want to make a speech at the reception because you hate speaking in public. But I'm talking about speaking in private." Skye sat taller. "So, can you promise me you'll speak up?"

Elsie's nose wrinkled. "That's a dangerous thing to ask. Tomorrow, the officiant is going to say, 'If anyone has any reason why these two shouldn't marry'?"

Skye arched her brows. "Yes! If you know Dan's got three secret families in other countries, and he's actually my half-brother who poisoned my grandmother's cat in an attempt to commit tax fraud—yes!"

Elsie rubbed her chin. "But if only half of that is true, I should just keep it to myself?" and Skye laughed. "You've watched too many soap operas."

"And you haven't watched enough of them." Skye hugged her. "I'm sorry I didn't read between the lines about Dan. But if you can be happy for me, that's enough."

"Do you forgive me?"

"I forgive you." Skye hugged her tighter. "And then we need to work on you forgiving Noah. Because I saw the two of you exchanging glances yesterday, and honestly, you're still really cute together."

CHAPTER FIFTEEN

Moving his flight up to tomorrow would cost an extra hundred-thirty-five dollars, but there was no reason to stay in Brighthead even one minute longer. If Noah could have moved it to tonight, he would have.

Lying on the bed in the rental unit, Noah muttered imprecations about the airline website while he hunted for earlier flights. It was slow and forced him to work through ten options every time he looked at a flight, only to tell him on the tenth screen that this flight was unavailable. At which point it booted him back to the first screen and happily asked him the identical nine questions.

Calling the airline directly was an even more unattractive option. He'd likely be on hold until the time of his original flight. It would be faster just to drive to the airport and ask at a desk there.

The only option so far, the hundred-thirty-five dollar one, involved Noah leaving the unit at four in the morning, and he didn't hate it here badly enough to stumble out of town an hour before the sun rose.

A knock on the door. Of course, the landlady would have heard him muttering at the website the whole time. She'd want to know if he was planning to abandon ship early, and he'd have to promise that yes, his credit card had gotten charged for the full number of days, and she'd have to trust him to have washed the cake pans and her liquid measuring cup.

Instead he found Dan at the door. "Nice place. I didn't know people could rent a rat-hole to tourists."

"The owner can hear every word you're saying, and it's not so much of a rat-hole that I couldn't use it as central headquarters for ruining your life."

Dan opened his hand. "Except you failed. If the owner's going to listen to everything we say, can we go somewhere else?"

Noah patted his pockets for his wallet and phone, as well as the unit key, then shut the door. "So it's easier to dump my body in the bay?"

"She would finger me to the cops in a heartbeat, and you know they'd listen to her because what else do the Brighthead police have to do?" Dan cupped his hands around his mouth. "Hello, Mrs. Edgemont!"

From upstairs came a muffled, "Hello, Daniel! Nice to see you!"

Noah sighed. Dan headed down the driveway with, "Follow me, Szymczak."

They didn't take Dan's car, which served as more collateral that Dan had no intention of leaving Noah in a dumpster. Dan said, "I confronted your partner in crime, and she confessed to everything, so you don't need to protect her anymore. Right now I'm mostly ticked off that you ruined the epic prank *she* had planned, which I'd have been telling my grandkids about."

Noah said, "I get why she pulled the plug."

"Yeah, but dude." Dan sighed. "Okay, so talk to me. We never met up again after you bolted out of Brighthead, so you never told me just how angry you were."

Noah sighed. "Really?"

"You were my partner in crime, and we pulled off the best senior prank in the history of senior pranks—and then you vanished on me. I'd text and you wouldn't reply, and then that summer I popped over to your house and found out you'd gone to live with your dad."

Noah said, "Which should have given you a clue."

"No, dude—I thought you'd gone to live with your dad because you wanted to live with your dad. And after that, you never came home again. But you're here now, so it's time to talk."

Noah shoved his hands in his pockets. Dan turned a corner, and now they were heading downhill, closer to town.

Dan said, "I apologized to Elsie, so I'm going to apologize to you, too. I had no idea that prank was going to be as big of a deal as it turned out to be. I didn't think your neighbors would call the cops. I didn't for a minute think it would break you up because everything looked okay from the outside. She loved a good prank, too, and I figured she'd laugh it off. Which, at the time, she seemed to. Neither of you got in major trouble, so I thought, no harm done."

Noah huffed. "I remember how you were back then. You wouldn't have apologized even if you'd known."

"But I'm apologizing now. I screwed up big time, and I can't make that up to you. Also, Elsie decided apparently she also stinks at communicating, because she realized she never told you Skye got left at the altar."

Noah shook his head.

Dan said, "Which is beside the fact that at the moment, she stinks at communicating with you specifically because she blocked you."

Noah's hands tightened. "Since you know everything already, why are you here?"

Dan stopped. "Look. You were my friend. We had awesome times together, and everything fell apart. You and I were like the dynamic duo, and I genuinely liked having you as my friend. I missed you."

Noah shook his head. "I didn't feel like I missed you. I felt betrayed by you."

"But it doesn't have to still be that way." Dan paused. "I want another chance. I want you and me again as partners in crime. I want your second cousins to pretend to arrest me while they leave a Towncar idling in the parking lot. I want to finally crack your social media passwords and post for the entire world that your height is not under discussion."

Noah snickered. "Dude, think of my job."

"The bigger the feather in my cap when I finally crack it."

"It's not going to happen." Noah shook his head. "You're still the same. The good parts, I mean."

Dan said, "Come to the wedding, tomorrow. Skye and I both want you there."

Noah said, "You didn't see the volley of texts I got from Elsie. If you don't throw me out, she's going to. And those guys in black aren't only going to idle in the parking lot with me tied up in the back seat."

Dan said, "I think she's into you again."

Noah rolled his eyes. "Pretty sure I blew that."

"Well, I blew everything eight years ago, and we're talking now." Dan pushed him on the shoulder. "Give it a chance. Come to the wedding. Just, tomorrow?"

Noah raised his hands. "Tomorrow, we're playing it straight. And I won't swap out your tuxedo for a child-sized tuxedo and say it shrank in the wash."

Dan flinched. "Oh, man. Now we've ruined two amazing pranks."

Noah shrugged. "You know me. I've barely gotten started." He sighed. "And tomorrow, I guess I'm trying to start over with Elsie. Again."

CHAPTER SIXTEEN

Elsie lay on her back at five in the morning while the first moments of sunrise brightened her room.

It was too easy to remember cuddling on her carpet with Noah, kissing him over a box of costumes. Then too easy to remember her outrage because he'd broken yet another promise. Tomorrow morning, Noah would go home, but today was the wedding, and Dan had talked Noah into staying.

Skye was right—they weren't communicating. She and Noah kept getting constrained by the things they weren't saying and the things they assumed. Or was it rather that when they dated, she'd kept waiting for Noah to read her mind? *If he really loved me, he'd know I don't want vanilla ice cream. If he really loved me, he'd invite me out to the pier tonight instead of talking to me on the phone.*

He *had* really loved her. He'd loved her enough to teach himself to read her mind—almost—and it was a dynamic that never would have worked. All along, Elsie had been declining to speak up. He'd made his best guesses based on what she hinted and how she reacted. Whenever she'd blown up at him over something (eg, when he'd gotten her a birthday gift but no card) then afterward, he'd corrected it (a Christmas card in her locker on the last day before break, and another one on her actual Christmas gift).

It worked. Except for when it didn't.

Eight years later, the minute they'd started things back up, she'd lapsed into the same dynamic. *Of course Noah could hear the things she wasn't saying. If he really loved her, he'd know all these things.*

Which was, in daylight, nonsense.

Noah hadn't returned to the dynamic. He hadn't listened past the words Elsie wasn't saying for all the things that were of vital importance. He'd asked her to speak up and be clear, and despite that, history had repeated. Noah had done what she said, and not what she wanted.

How could a relationship like that last long-distance? When a long-distance relationship was almost entirely communication?

Although, really, even a face-to-face relationship was mostly communication.

Staying broken up was for the best. With all these half-truths and the expectation of mind-reading, how could they survive?

It wasn't just romantic relationships: Skye had accused Elsie of the same thing: how could Skye have known how badly Dan had hurt her? *If you were really my friend, you'd know how angry I still was.* And then it turned out Noah had done basically the same thing: Noah had read Dan's mind via his behavior, and concluded Dan was never a friend in the first place.

Elsie could communicate just fine with the horses. She paid attention to their motions, to their mood. To the very tiniest movements of their noses and ears. Moreover, she didn't expect the horses to read her mind—no, with an animal that big, you approached from where you were visible and made all your intentions very obvious, and when you spoke, you kept your commands clear.

Elsie also communicated well with her clients, several of whom were themselves nonverbal. She kept it simple. Direct. But she also didn't expect any of them to meet her emotional needs because that's not what clients are for—and that wasn't what horses are for.

For years, Elsie had avoided the spotlight, avoided attention, avoided standing up for herself. But was she humble—or was she timid? Taking a stand meant committing and then holding to that commitment. It meant people knew exactly who you were—but it also meant you had to know who you were, yourself. Getting recognized meant first having an identity.

Working with the horses, again, it was easy. If you didn't know who was in charge in the ring, the horse would put itself in charge, and you were in trouble. But in her own life, Elsie kept slipping away from any situation where she had to speak up because that meant making a firm decision—and too often, she felt soft inside. Uncertain. She didn't want to own up to any particular opinion, and she cloaked it as being shy.

Even when she wanted to prank Dan, she'd made it Noah's project, so she didn't have to be in charge.

Maybe the problem wasn't even Elsie not knowing how to communicate as much as Elsie not knowing herself.

She flipped on her side. Five-fifteen. The room was bright now. She reached for her phone and unblocked Noah. "I need to talk to you."

He replied, "I'm awake."

Why did he always respond so quickly? For that matter, why was he even awake in that basement apartment where surely the light couldn't have squeaked into any of the windows through the bushes? "I'm sorry I blew up at you yesterday. I didn't realize I hadn't told you Skye's history."

He replied, "Apology accepted."

Mind-reading was off the table, but that text read like a man simmering with anger. Elsie texted, "Skye and I talked last night. She thinks I never tell everyone what I mean, and that causes problems."

Noah said, "Is she right?"

In the interests of clarity, Elsie didn't reply, "Is this a cross-examination?" and instead texted, "Yes."

Noah said, "So it's an empathy thing? You assume people know things just because you know them?"

Elsie frowned at the screen. "Your degree is in psychology?"

"Wasn't aware one requires a degree to talk to you."

Again, even in the absence of mind-reading, that sounded angry. "Maybe it is an empathy thing. Skye made me promise to say everything I mean from now on."

Noah sent a string of emoji faces ranging from puzzled to laughing to slightly sarcastic.

"Well, I'm going to try."

He texted, "Good luck." Then, "Dan said he pretended I implicated you. I didn't. I told him it was all me."

"Yeah, he's still a deceptive little snake."

"Your cousins should have arrested him after all."

"No kidding." She sent that, then, "I'm glad you're still coming to the wedding."

No reply at first. Elsie sat cross-legged in bed, listening for the waves out at low tide, then checking the forecast. Skye had been freaking out (six months ago) that the weather would be lousy, as if any of them could have done anything about that. "No, I'm totally calm," Skye had said, fists clenched and eyes wide, "but what if there's a hurricane?" in a state where a hurricane hadn't landed in thirty-one years.

Elsie had shown Skye the tent rental places and calculated how many human bodies could fit into her mother's house, and she'd drawn diagrams for how to set up the wedding of Skye's dreams even during a scenario of nightmares.

Except—that hadn't been Elsie's first response. Elsie's first response had been to think of tent rentals and the basement square footage and then tell Skye, "We'll make it work." It was only when nonspecific reassurances resulted in Skye getting even more worked up that Elsie had pulled up the rental website and drawn the diagrams.

Elsie texted again, "Can I have a dance with you before you leave?"

Noah replied, "Sure."

Elsie wasn't being totally honest right now. Did she want one dance with Noah—or did she want twenty? She wanted to kiss him—but did she want to start things again, or did she want to kiss him goodbye?

How can you tell people what you want when you don't know it, yourself?

And for that matter, how can you give away your heart when you never fully made it your own?

———⊙⊙———

Noah looked great. He'd always looked great when he dressed up (gosh, remember his prom tuxedo? And how Elsie had bragged he'd look equally amazing at her wedding?) but even in a suit, he looked pretty darned amazing. She caught a look at him when she processed in at the end of the line of bridesmaids.

He glanced at her, but not with the amazement she wanted, and it surprised her again—surprised her that she wanted him amazed. They had no future, so why should he give her a jaw-dropped stare, or a smirk with his eyebrows raised?

Then Skye arrived up the center aisle, Dan watched with his eyes huge and a broad smile across his lips. And Elsie knew that: that was the look she had wanted from Noah.

Despite the lack of an official rehearsal, everyone made it through. Kevin's oversimplification was right: ninety-nine percent of a wedding was the same from event to event. Skye and Dan had chosen all the parts of the wedding they wanted, and the officiant had reviewed it with them even before the rehearsal-that-never-was.

The guests had seats on the beach, and the bride and

groom stood on a platform over the rocks with the ocean at their backs. The couple exchanged their vows with the waves hushing in and out of the bay, and an ocean bird circling just over the edge of the water.

"Present the rings," said the officiant, and Kevin didn't pat down his pockets while looking horrified. The ring went onto Skye's finger, and then another one onto Dan's. The bride and groom kissed, and Elsie couldn't applaud because she was laden with her bouquet and Skye's—but she wanted to.

Dan was a good guy, after all. He was good for Skye.

The caterers unveiled the food, and everyone dispersed beneath the tents to sit at their different tables while the DJ started the music. Elsie set her bouquet at the head table, and then she looked up to find Noah. He said, "Did you mean it about that dance?"

She smoothed her pale pink bridesmaid's gown. "Assuming I can dance in this thing."

"I'd tell you to take off your heels, but then you'd be all the way down there." He grinned as she glared with her hands on her hips. "Everything went well."

Elsie said, "You're leaving tomorrow morning?"

"Nine-fifteen." He shrugged. "My boss would get testy if I never returned. And you have your hippos to therapy."

She opened her hands. "I can't work remotely. For some reason."

Noah glanced about. "The house has enough property. You could fit a horse in the garage and then walk it around the waterfront."

"On all the rocks," she said. "That will do great for both the horse and the client."

The DJ played Skye and Dan's first dance. It was not— still not—the Edgar Chantz ballad.

Kevin approached. "Maid of Honor Elsie Jenner, are you still refusing to give a speech?"

Elsie made a mock bow. "All yours, Best Man Kevin."

Noah turned to Elsie. "I think you should."

"Not giving a speech was the only thing I asked Skye

before I agreed to be Maid of Honor."

"Figures."

Kevin laughed. "Still world-famous for not liking attention. Well, fortunately, some people do like attention, and I plan to give it to them."

Elsie narrowed her eyes. Noah said, "Not to Elsie. Not unless you want to find out whether your damage deposit gets returned after that tux is doused in salt water."

"Touchy! No, it won't involve Elsie," and he turned as Jen joined him with a kiss and her arms around his shoulders.

Noah led Elsie away by the arm before she got a chance to roll her eyes at Kevin. Noah murmured, "He does know it's a violation of every social norm to propose at someone else's wedding?"

"Everyone knows that." She shrugged. "As long as I don't have to make a speech, I don't care what he's planning."

Noah said, "But if you gave a speech, at least it would be an honest speech."

Elsie shuddered. "And yet, really, not something anyone can convince me to do."

From behind came a shouted, "You two!" Elsie turned just as her grandmother marched up to them with her walker. "Aren't you Noah, the brat who made Elsie cry right before she went to college?"

Elsie's cheeks went pinker than her dress, but Noah only bowed. "The same, Mrs. Jenner. How have you been?"

She poked him. "A lot better before you arrived here. Come with me. I need to go through the buffet line, and you have two hands."

Chastened, Noah followed her while Elsie bit her lip to stifle the giggles. *I didn't need a rescue this time,* she thought to her grandmother. *He wasn't about to kiss me.*

Which thought, again, tingled through Elsie with a momentary regret.

But still, Noah was so adorable, standing with her grandmother, Grandma pointing to each tray where she wanted something and Noah dutifully adding it for her.

After Noah carried Grandma's plate back to her table,

Elsie made sure she had everything she needed. Grandma huffed. "All this fuss over me. At a place with all this food, and you're standing around not eating!"

Dismissed, Elsie accompanied Noah through the line on his second pass-through, although he didn't serve up food onto her plate. The buffet was luxurious, the tents breezy while sheltering them from the sun. Elsie pulled up a chair at Noah's table rather than at the head table. Skye wasn't there, anyhow. She was making rounds of the entire roster of wedding guests.

It was over. In a few hours, the caterers would have packed up, and Skye and Dan would be driving to the airport. Months of planning, fulfilled.

Then in the morning, Noah would be gone, too.

Which, well—there wasn't a choice.

Elsie stopped herself: she was supposed to be honest about what she said. She *was* making a choice. She was choosing to let him go rather than choosing to doom them to months of miscommunication and get her heart broken a second time.

Also, Noah had made his own choice: he was choosing to go home. Since she wanted him to respect her rules, she had to respect his, as well.

Noah followed her gaze out toward the ocean. "What are you thinking?"

Elsie didn't look away from the waves. "In the interests of my new commitment to honesty in speech, I'm not going to tell you."

"Ah, one of those thoughts." He didn't make it sound salacious, but he could just about almost kind of read her mind, so he likely knew what she was thinking.

The DJ started a slow song, and Noah extended a hand. "I do believe it's time to discharge my dance obligation."

"Dear heaven, the romance just steams off you." Elsie fanned herself. "How can a girl resist?"

On the dance floor laid out over the rocks, Dan and Skye along with a number of other couples were already swaying with their arms around one another. Noah found a clearing and then put his arms around Elsie. She rested one hand behind his neck and the other on his forearm.

Eight years. Then one blip, and he'd be gone again. Elsie fought the urge to rest her head against his shoulder. Noah still moved with the same gentle sway, the same easy pressure on the small of her back.

He looked sad. She said, "Your turn. What are you thinking?"

"I'm thinking your grandmother's going to make me dance with her instead."

Elsie snorted a laugh.

Noah said, "She'll tear me from your arms, and that will be a shame."

Elsie said, "There will be other dances "

Noah said, "You're supposed to be honest today, not just saying what you think I want to hear."

That ended conversation. Couples in Jane Austen novels could banter during bizarrely complicated dances, but not Elsie and Noah. And Noah was right: after today, there would be no more dances.

After the slow dance, the DJ told everyone to get back to their seats because it was time for the toast. Elsie abandoned Noah and took her place at the head table. Kevin stood holding the mic.

Smirking.

What was he up to?

Kevin began the speech by talking about how long he'd known Dan, and what a prankster Dan had always been. Terrific: Dan had told *Noah* not to prank the reception, but he hadn't told Kevin, and what was Kevin about to do? Set off a confetti cannon?

Kevin started talking about true love, and Elsie caught sight of his girlfriend, Jen, sitting on the edge of her seat—looking expectant.

No. Absolutely not.

Elsie sought out Skye's eyes, but Skye was looking only at Kevin, not recognizing the bigger picture. So was Dan. No way to warn them to cut him off. It was a wireless mic, too—no way to pull the plug.

She looked to Noah, who wore a dark anger. Okay, so Elsie wasn't over-reacting. Kevin was definitely setting up a proposal.

Kevin walked around the table to Jen, and Elsie looked desperately for a glass of soda she could dump in Jen's lap by accident—except everything had been cleared off already.

Kevin got on one knee, and Skye shot Elsie a horrified look.

Elsie stood.

Kevin said into the mic, "Jen, will you marry me?"

Elsie exclaimed, "Kevin, you were supposed to marry me!"

Total chaos. There were laughs and exclamations, and Jen pivoted to stare at Elsie. In fact, everyone was staring, but it didn't kill her. Their eyes—their attention—weren't going to kill her.

She was going to take a stand for something: and that something was protecting Skye.

Elsie marched over to Kevin to pluck the mic from his hands. She turned to one of the other groomsmen. "John, since Kevin's being a prat, will *you* marry me?"

Laughing, John took the mic from Elsie and faced one of the guests. "Casey, I've known you for twenty years, and weddings are so romantic. Will you marry me?"

Kevin looked aghast, and Jen was white as a sheet, but Skye was laughing with her hands over her mouth. Elsie rushed over to intercept the mic, and she got down on one knee in front of the ring bearer. "Timmy, you did a great job carrying the rings. Will you marry me?"

Timmy's father didn't need the mic to project his voice. "Give him sixteen years, and that's a solid maybe."

One of Dan's cousins seized the mic from Elsie's hand and bowed to Elsie's grandmother. "Mrs. Jenner, in honor of the day, may I humbly ask your hand in marriage?"

Grandma snorted. "You did a better job of asking than that first man! Go refill my drink," and she handed him the cup.

Noah snatched the mic from the groomsman. "I'll be taking bids for my own hand in marriage at www-dot-my-hand-in-marriage-dot-com, where I've listed my complete qualifications to serve as husband for any willing participant, including my salary projections for the next five years and a link to my stock profile."

Elsie howled with laughter. By now Kevin and Jen's attempted wedding hijack was well and truly in flames. Dan's uncle took the mic from Noah. In a voice used to command, he intoned, "I'm an off-duty police officer, and the first person to propose marriage to the flower girl gets arrested. Remember, you're on video."

The flower girl's older sister, and Skye's junior bridesmaid, took the mic and knelt before a guest's service dog, a Schipperke. "Polywoly, you're a good dog! The goodest dog ever!" The dog's tail wagged fast enough to beat the ocean breeze. "Polywoly, will you marry me?"

Polywoly licked the junior bridesmaid's face, and everyone applauded. She dropped the mic to bury her arms in the dog's fur.

Kevin strode toward the discarded mic, but Elsie and Noah both darted forward to secure the mic before Kevin could. Although Kevin would have to be an idiot to repeat his proposal right now, Elsie wasn't sure exactly how big of an idiot he was.

Elsie dropped to her knees and grabbed the mic half a second before Noah would have gotten it, and they ended up face to face, her on one knee, looking up at him where he stood over her.

Elsie said into the mic, "Noah, we had a horrible false start eight years ago, but I've never forgotten you. I'm so glad you're back in my life, and I don't want to let you go again. We need to learn to communicate better, but there's nothing here we can't work out. Will you marry me?"

Today was the day for honesty, right? Total honesty.

Eyes wide, Noah stammered, "I have some reservations, but sure, why not?"

She could hardly breathe. Noah gentled the mic away from her and then turned toward Kevin. "Sorry, dude, you're out of luck—I'm already spoken for." He pounded Kevin on the shoulder. "Everyone, let's have a round of applause for Kevin, pranking the prankster on the best day of his life!"

Noah raised his hands, and everyone applauded. Kevin did not look as if he appreciated this, and he stalked back toward the head table where Jen was pointedly glaring away—and Dan was pointedly glaring at him.

Noah turned toward the head table where Skye sat looking surprised—but relieved. He grabbed the nearest champagne glass and raised it. "To marriage, the biggest decision any of us will make." He kept the glass raised, then added, "And from all of us who've finally had our hearts' desire made clear to us—congratulations to the bride and groom!"

EPILOGUE

Elsie gave in to a fit of giggles as she opened her closet and found hanging there not her wedding gown, but a similar gown, toddler-sized.

Skye cried out, "Oh, no! It shrank in the wash!"

Before Mom's horrified eyes, Elsie removed the miniature dress from layers of plastic, then unbuttoned the back. "I'll hold my breath and pull it on. It'll be fine."

She flared out the multiple layers at the bottom, then peeked through the neck hole (careful not to muss her updo or her makeup) and Skye took a photo.

Mom exclaimed, "Where's the actual dress?" and Skye sashayed from the room to retrieve it from wherever she'd hidden it. Five minutes later, Elsie stood in a white tea-length gown with an illusion lace neckline and embroidered flowers. She tied on her white bridal sneakers with lacy laces, and then let Skye secure her hairpiece.

Perfect for a backyard wedding, especially when your backyard was a rocky beach.

After two years of hosting weddings at the beach house, Mom had the process down pat, but she was still nervous. She adjusted Elsie's hairpiece, then got the bridesmaids set up with their flowers.

Elsie snuck a peek out the window. Noah was downstairs with the groomsmen and the officiant. Dan was pacing close to the shore holding the baby.

Skye said, "Are you ready?"

The weather wasn't as gorgeous as it had been for Skye's wedding, but then again, with a wedding hashtag like #BluettSkyes, the weather wouldn't have dared be cloudy. Today was breezier, and passing clouds would cut the heat. Mom cued the musicians to start, and out went the bridesmaids, followed by Skye as the Maid of Honor, and then Elsie processed in at the end.

Noah got a first look at her, beaming. She joined him on the platform, gripping his hand as if that ocean breeze were going to blow one of them away.

They'd worked hard for this. Two years of training themselves to communicate better, of learning to read between their own lines rather than trying to hear what the other wasn't saying. They'd even taken an online class in how to speak with each other—and it wasn't perfect. But it was working. When Noah had finally said, "Will you marry me?" it had been after eighteen months of heart-to-heart talks, lots of listening, and learning to negotiate to find common ground.

Which led to here, the common ground of a platform on a rocky beach, with the ocean before them and their loved ones at their back, and their hands clasped to one another.

Here they said something else honest: that they vowed to love, honor, and cherish one another for as long as they both shall live.

The officiant said, "I now pronounce you man and wife!"

Noah and Elsie turned to face everyone, and then both burst out laughing.

All the wedding guests were wearing masks that looked like either Elsie's face or Noah's.

Except for Dan, who was wearing an Edgar Chantz mask, and holding a guitar.

Elsie laughed as she threw her arms around Noah, and still grinning, he kissed the bride.

THANK YOU!

Thank you so much for reading about Noah and Elsie! These two were a lot of fun to write, and I hope you had just as much fun reading about them.

Remember: pranks are awesome, but only if everyone can laugh afterward. Also, if you've never had a cat litter cake, there are a dozen recipes online, and some of them look far too realistic for comfort.

I'd like to thank my early readers, without whom Grandma wouldn't have been at the wedding. All your input helped make the story so much better.

If you're interested in hearing more from me, every week I put together a newsletter called Maddie Monday, where I share a weird tidbit from my life as well as a recommendation—maybe a book I've enjoyed or a knitting pattern. If you're interested, please sign up at https://stats.sender.net/forms/erBXBe/view.

THE SUMMER VACATION ROMANCE SERIES

Twelve books, twelve vacation destinations, twelve different couples who are about to escape from their everyday routine into the greatest adventure of the rest of their lives.

From awkward double-bookings to second chances, from daydreamers to wounded hearts, the Summer Vacation Romances will sweep you up in the surprise and delight of new love.

The Summer Vacation Romance novellas are sweet romances that will transport your heart to the getaway of your dreams. Each book stands alone, so you can book your escape in any order you like. Bon voyage!

The four members of a string quartet tune up to play and tune in to their hearts. Violist Ashlyn learned to express herself only after she was adopted into a family of musicians—but now a handsome man has come along claiming he's also a member of the family, himself given up for adoption. Hannah, the cellist, reaches out to Enrique, vocalist and longtime friend, for help when a stalker upends her life, only to discover falling in love can upend it even more. And the first and second violinists are forced to work together despite their longtime feud, only to discover they have far more in common than they ever anticipated.

Heart of the Violist
Soul of the Cellist
Spirit of the Violinists

Learn how life, love, and loss intermingle in the Castleton String Quartet Romances, a sweet small-town romance trilogy.

www.ingramcontent.com/pod-product-compliance
Lightning Source LLC
Chambersburg PA
CBHW030309130626
46549CB00002B/772